BOOK 1 OF THE SERIES
THE ORDER OF UTOPIA

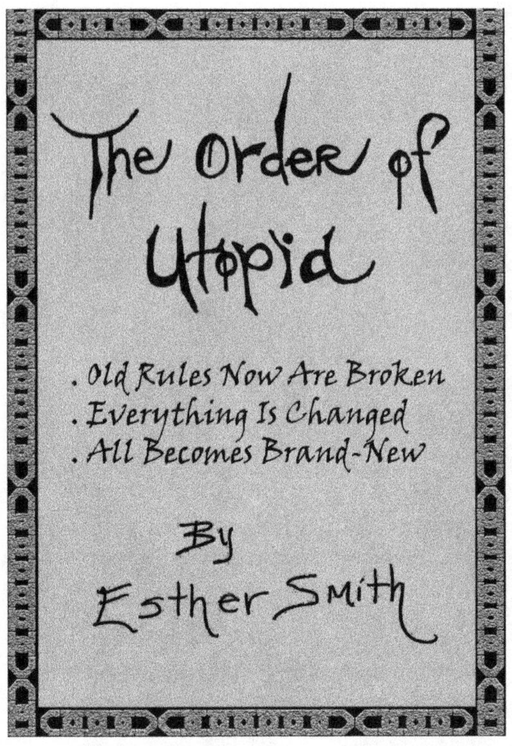

—First Edition—

ISBN 978-1-59433-998-1
eBook ISBN 978-1-59433-999-8

Library of Congress Catalog Card Number: 2020951618

Book 1 designed by Esther Smith

Publication Consultants
HTTP://WWW.PUBLICATIONCONSULTANTS.COM

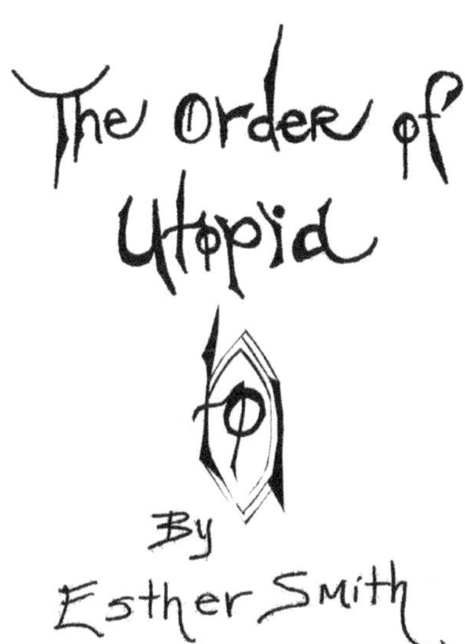

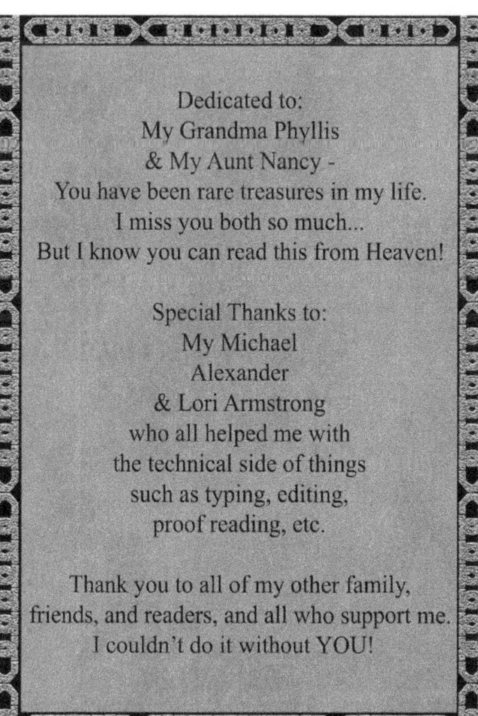
Dedicated to:
My Grandma Phyllis
& My Aunt Nancy -
You have been rare treasures in my life.
I miss you both so much...
But I know you can read this from Heaven!

Special Thanks to:
My Michael
Alexander
& Lori Armstrong
who all helped me with
the technical side of things
such as typing, editing,
proof reading, etc.

Thank you to all of my other family,
friends, and readers, and all who support me.
I couldn't do it without YOU!

Lorraina Parsons
Age: 23
Birth Gender: Female
Natural Hair Color: Brown
Complexion: Fair
Personality: Rebel
Height: 5'6"
Weight: 139

WORLD CATALOGING PROGRAM

ONE ORDER

Krista Guthrie
Age: 23
Birth Gender: Female
Natural Hair Color: Black
Complexion: Dark
Personality: Rebel
Height: 5'8"
Weight: 151

Richard Perecha
Age: 68
Birth Gender: Male
Natural Hair Color: Black
Complexion: Medium
Personality: Rebel
Height: 6’2”
Weight: 211

WORLD CATALOGING PROGRAM

ONE ORDER

Hayden Baulmfield
Age: 33
Birth Gender: Male
Natural Hair Color: Blonde
Complexion: Fair
Personality: Unknown
Height: 5’11”
Weight: 185

Liam Heepen
Age: 11
Birth Gender: Male
Natural Hair Color: L.Bro
Complexion: Fair
Personality: Unknown
Height: 4’4”
Weight: 87

WORLD CATALOGING PROGRAM

NE ORDER

Bridget Buchannon
Age: 25
Birth Gender: Female
Natural Hair Color: Ginger
Complexion: Fair
Personality: Passive
Height: 5’5”
Weight: 148

Jarom Freeman
Age: 27
Birth Gender: Male
Natural Hair Color: Black
Complexion: Medium
Personality: Unknown
Height: 6’0”
Weight: 192

WORLD CATALOGING PROGRAM

ONE ORDER

Howard Heepen
Age: 60
Birth Gender: Male
Natural Hair Color: D. Bro
Complexion: Medium
Personality: Unknown
Height: 6’1”
Weight: 190

CHAPTER 1

Bubbling over with arrogance, confidence, ego and obsession for his field, Hayden Baulmfield presented a follow up address on his thesis. He began speaking just after the microphones evened out and stopped their screeching and static, and as a hush went across the enormous audience.

"Ladies and gentlemen, fellow citizens – on this rare 'once in a lifetime occasion' – let us make it one to never forget. You guys... Rex is ALIVE!" his voice elevated and grew more dramatic and intense.

"Many of you skeptics and elitists..." Hayden went on, now speaking down to his audience, "Have your arrogant attitudes and hold on to your disdain for me, due primarily to my 'huge' following" he boasted. "You're only here because you want to watch me fail and glory in my failure, but I got news for you. I'm gloating right now, because I can see some of you squirming in your seats... I am NOT failing, am I? You don't even need to answer that, because if you look around, you should be able to see for yourselves!" Hayden paused for a moment of silence using his arm to sweep out and display the décor all about the conference center.

Palm fronds, cycad, gingko, cinnamon ferns and many other live vegetation species that were common to the Cretaceous period abounded prolifically in the décor throughout the room. No expense was considered too great in the preparations for this event.

Tables were draped with elegant rich toned burgundy and gray table cloths, representing the colors of Tyrannosaurus Rex's exterior and interior. The walls were also draped, but they were covered with crinkled Tapa-cloth and woven beige fabrics.

Each table was set out with full formal china settings and with silver platters of grapes and cheeses. Real silver silverware had been set and every table had plates topped with a silver bell shaped covering known as a cloche, for every attendee.

Ammonites, trilobites, conches, and other shells lay randomly about the tables near the main center piece, which was a very large T-Rex claw on the center of every table.

"Well, for all you doubters..." Hayden began again with another pause and smirk on his face. "For all of my fans, for everyone in between... I could have never afforded this luxurious setting or meal, if we didn't hit it off big!"

He stood beaming, his smile using every muscle in his neck and face. "So... enjoy your amazing meal and then for the conclusion, the climax, we will give the details of our discoveries. So, eat up, enjoy! Come up with all of your questions; jot them down... because I'll take questions following the meal. Thank you!" he concluded bowing as the crowd cheered and clapped with utter excitement.

Music began to play. This music, the guests of the event, recognized as being the thematic music from various dinosaur movies. Other instrumental climatic background music played in the background as well. Light strands and nets got a little brighter as they were lowered from the high ceiling closer to the tables as people were sitting down to eat.

A giant screen like a movie theater, covering the entire back of the stage Hayden had been standing on, began to show gorgeous footage and scenery of exotic landscapes. Waiters in black tuxedos with red and grey bolo ties that looked more like scarves, came around to every table and removed the cloche covering from each of the silver platters revealing a gigantic nine pound steak, grilled and sizzling with pepper and Cajun spices, mushrooms all around, cubed potatoes, asparagus, all drizzled with butter, parsley and honey.

The aroma was incredible and astounding upon everyone's nostrils. Many sounds of shock and amazement were audible throughout the large crowd of over 100 tables. All could clearly see, and were reminded with signs that read "No amount of funding was spared" when it came to the ambiance and overall setting of the dinner and backdrop for the speaker.

The attendees devoured large portions of their food. Salads with great olives and seeds came out to each table every time they were emptied, as well as buttered garlic breads.

When every person was full, and could eat no more, tables were cleared away. Not one person had been able to finish the gargantuan steaks and all of the food set out. Flawlessly, and almost in sync, each individual was served another silver platter with a cloche on top of it.

"Do not yet open your dessert until I say" Hayden began again thematically as the music had faded away gradually. "I will now take questions, for those who have prepared them. If I deem the questions ridiculous, then I will ignore you and say, 'Moving on', if they are worth answering I'll answer them."

Hayden continued, now over the top with arrogance and utter ego in his mannerisms and body language. "Taking question number one... you in the green dress" he said pointing to a woman in the crowd.

She had light brown and auburn hair and dark brown eyes and was fairly plain with no makeup, freckles lightly sprinkling all visible flesh, and a mid to large size nose. She didn't seem to fit in with the rest of the crowd Hayden had noticed and was curious.

Her clothes were unique; her entire appearance was very distinguishable, but not specifically in a glamorous or flashy way. She wore a solid, high necked tunic with braided rope designs running vertically down the dress on a solid black velvet, inlay, stripe about 8 inches across running down to the floor the entire length of the gown.

A thick, heavy woolen cloak was wrapped around her shoulders from around her back over her biceps bunching at her sides and draped down along side of the queen-like regalia. This mesmerized Hayden. She was in her late 40s and Hayden was just over 30, it was not a typical physical attraction, but almost as if a spell had overtaken him.

Hayden barely blinked as he stared with curiosity; this was now visible to the entire audience.

"Your name..." he paused briefly, then blinked and snapped out of it a little, realizing everyone could see his sort of trance. "Please state your name, where you are from, who you represent, and then your question." He concluded gesturing for her to speak.

She stood slowly, shyly picking up the microphone from the assistant handing it to her. "I am from another time, not yours. I have come to warn you. My name is Tyrnia ***(Teer-nee-uh)***, The Woman of Woes. I am a messenger of warnings" she went on.

"I say woe unto all who force, coerce, deceive, and make afraid, be wise, cautious, and prudent. Do not let your love for glory, pride and proof, be your downfall."

"Is there a question in all of this, Teary Woman?" Hayden mocked smartly in a quick flippant manner.

"The question is, will the world heed a warning, will this group heed a warning, will any who can hear the sound of my voice heed this warning, especially... will you... heed a warning?"

"Moving on!" Hayden blurted sarcastically.

"You with the hat sir" Hayden pointed out a tall, thin young man with a typical suit for such a black tie occasion, but strangely enough he was wearing a brightly decorated sombrero with little, red, pompom balls dangling around from all of the edges. As the microphone got to him, the graceful Tyrnia made her way as quietly as possible to the exit in the back.

"So, how do you know 'Rex is alive' Mr. Baulmfield? Do you have any proof or evidence... or is this all just expensive talk?"

"That is the question I have been waiting for!" Hayden held his hands up to the sky in a powerful, 'glory to me' sort of manner.

"Yes!" He said, "Yes, yes, perfect! Questions are already over" he continued. "I hoped for this question, so that now I can give you dessert. So... now for your proof!" he said boldly. "You want proof??? You got it!" Hayden finished, signaling with his arms in an upward motion demonstrating for the waiters to remove the cloches.

"Don't do it!" Tyrnia yelled out, turning back towards the main room, looking Hayden in the eyes across the entire building in a piercing, fiery way that seemed to dart across the room, in an aggressive, ferocious, defensive manner. "Do not lift those lids!" she demanded in a commanding, authority seldom found, which seemed to speak to those who were present's minds, without even using words.

"Remove the cloches now!" Hayden barked back, ordering his workers. All the waiters removed the cloche plate covers simultaneously, revealing the tiny 6- 12 inch miniature baby dinosaurs.

"What amazing slumbering creatures" an excited guest shouted out to Hayden, "Can we touch them?"

Each person leaned forward for a closer look. They were beautiful in their own right and from a scientific accomplishment standpoint, they were incredible, and what 'should' be impossible, but there they were.

As Tyrnia turned her head in disgust, and walked out of the exit, Hayden responded all the louder, hoping that she could hear him, annoyed that she would dare tell him what to do. "Feel free to gently touch them, at your own risk!" he spoke over the loud speaker.

Remarkable variance of blues, grey and reds faded into one another with snake like textures and unique raised peaks all over the back and spines of the tiny creatures. The bumps were similar to a pointed broccoli/cauliflower type plant called a Romanesco broccoli. Appearing like miniscule volcanoes dotting the ridgeline of the infant creatures backs.

Each visitant was in awe, staring, gaping, some of them reaching out ever so frailly, unable to resist touching, since Mr. Baulmfield had given them permission.

"These can't be real!" a dark haired man called out from the audience. "This is too amazing to be real. You're tricking us somehow." He stated standing up and stepping back. "What was that strange woman's warning about?" he began sweating and getting antsy and panic flushed over his entire demeanor and conduct.

"Oh, they're real all right!" Hayden responded smartly.

"What will you do with them all, once they grow up? If they grow up!" a woman on the other side of the room began to wonder out loud. "What if they have health problems? How are they so tiny? I thought that T-Rex infants would be bigger" she continued her barrage of questions.

"Well, Madam, you thought wrong. And yes they can grow up, and no they don't have health problems, and they are so tiny because we cross bred them with chickens, so that we can manhandle them for various reasons. And at least you have some good thought provoking questions."

"Yes, Tyrannosaurus Rex infants are larger when we don't crossbreed them, but they taste better this way... mixed with chicken that is."

"Taste better?" a wiry old man snapped in disgust. "Why would you want to create something so amazing, just to destroy it?"

"Well, let me ask you" Hayden began... "Did it taste better? How did you like it? You can feed a lot of people with a T-Rex and you can grow T-Rex meat pretty fast too. But seriously... how did you enjoy your T-Rex meat dinner?"

"You mean we ate them?" said an old woman who nearly fainted and held her mouth in disgust, nearly throwing up at the thought. "Was that our steaks?" she let go of her mouth, long enough to ask.

"Yes, of course! I can't believe you didn't figure that out sooner... and where do you think the claws came from on the tables?" Hayden asked them rhetorically.

The dinosaurs began awaking with all of the oohing and awing people were giving them. They started blinking eyes and sat up and stared and look around at their immediate surroundings.

"Can you control them?" hollered the nervous young man in the sombrero and out of fear, as one baby T-Rex began arising and standing up.

"We surely can control them; in fact, we found that we can control them through a series of whistles and various dog calls. We are still testing things certainly, and experimenting but we are doing quite well and it was time to show the world."

Some people began to get very hesitant and set the cloches back over the babies, being overcome with excitement and adrenaline simultaneously, but having their reasoning over take them. Some people began to get up and walk out. Others looked confused and concerned. Many others were still too enthusiastic and were getting absurd dollar-signs stuck in their eyes, metaphorically speaking.

"Who's interested in partnering with me, in moving forward in a way that will change and bless the world forever?" Hayden said, and then awaited a response fleetingly.

"Anyone interested?" Hayden blurted out on the loud speaker once more. "I have so much more to show you behind this wall. We can take a tour right here, right now, today!" Hayden proclaimed. "Who's with me?" he said elevating his voice.

Many people raised hands, stood up, and began to walk toward him and where he was gesturing behind stage. "Come, I'll show you the new world."

Other individuals began to walk toward the exit doors. "You can't leave yet guys and gals" Hayden instructed them. "Come back and sit down".

"Unfortunately, we can't be having little live dinosaurs growing up out of controlled environments; one of you could have pocketed one. I will have to check you to ensure that this does not happen."

After he got all of the people who wanted to follow him to go up and wait behind the stage, which were over half of the guests, he said, "let the walk-through begin" in an exuberant manner and voice pitch.

The doors all unexpectedly locked and peculiar whistling and vibrating began throughout the room. All the baby T-Rex's sat up alertly, looked wide awake, and sprang to their feet.

Instantly, they lost all looks of cuteness and all feelings of endearment. There was hunger, thirst, and hunting in their eyes. They were genetically engineered to be predators.

One little infant dinosaur began walking slowly toward the man in the sombrero. The man backed up gently, and with no warning the T-Rex sprang off of the table at him.

It began biting and gnawing at his finger intensely. "Owe! Owe! Ahhhh! Arrrr!" the man was trying to deal with the pain and get the dinosaur away at the same time. Just then many of the babies leapt at the people that had been just shortly before, admiring their mere creation and beauty.

"Attack!" Hayden hollered loudly and began to laugh hysterically as he observed the pain that the dinosaurs were inflicting.

Screams and shrieks were echoing and bouncing throughout the giant building and people were dying. One man dropped right at Hayden's feet and he merely began laughing hysterically, even cackling.

Then the *Woman of Woe*, Tyrnia's voice echoed through the room, louder than the cries of help. "What's so funny? Why are you laughing?" Tyrnia called out from above Hayden's head, as if on an intercom system.

Looking up at the sky Hayden was confused. The whistling and vibrations increased as did the dinosaurs aggressions until one of his creations came at him. He began to run but it was faster than he'd anticipated. It bit at his ankles, pulling at his pant leg. It began to bite through the pant leg and he began kicking it.

"Get off, get off!" he shrieked and fell to the ground. It hopped right onto his chest and looked him in the eyes. When it had stared him down a little longer, it dove at his face and began licking him.

"What?" He freaked out and was relieved at the same time. He opened his eyes and saw his dog, Parkington.

His mom asked again, "What's so funny? You were laughing hysterically. I recorded you while you slept. I should upload it for everyone to see." She teased.

"Would you please shut your phone alarm off first though?" she asked. "That whistling is very annoying and it almost vibrated right off of the table… Also, I'm trying to get some laundry done and you are actually lying on top of all the clean laundry, I left down here on the couch".

Hayden's mother let out a deep sigh and burst out a little miffed, "Now I'm going to have to wash it all again today, because you didn't even shower or get out of your digging clothes and you soiled them, and stunk them all up sleeping on top of them like that".

She continued, "I know you love to stay over when you get done with your big digs and expeditions, and I love that you still want to, at your age, but you are definitely going to be helping with this laundry mister."

CHAPTER 2

"Doesn't anyone care to do more than this?" Lorraina sighed as she drew in a deep breath. "Nobody is even going to look up or respond?" she continued in an ever growing frustration. "All you guys ever want to do is watch movies, maybe play a few games, and stare at your stupid devices".

Nearly deafening silence permeated the air, and still no response from her roommates. All that could be heard was a slight sniffle, gulp, tapping of a screen, shuffling of sitting positions, and the sound of a rerun that was on Its third round that month alone.

"Well, I think I was created for something better than this. You are all my 'supposed' friends, and yet what do I get from you... an occasional glance, an eye roll, a gag sound? You don't offer even so much as an 'I'm sorry you feel that way' or a 'we'll miss you'.

Well, I can find better, and I can do better!

"I'm done begging for people to give me attention, or to look up at me every once in a while. There's gotta be somebody out there left, who likes to do something every once in a while, instead of just watching others live out their lives while you do nothing but rot" Lorraina paused and took a breath momentarily.

"Holy Wow!!!" she continued, raising her voice in an exacerbated manner. "Even now, even a goodbye isn't enough to get any of your attention! Well, I am utterly convinced then... been nice knowing you all!" she went on sarcastically.

"My bags are packed and if any of you even bothered to look away from your 'waste of time entertainment' for two seconds, you'd notice that they are in my hands".

A few of Lorraina's roommates finally glanced up half-heartedly, and one girl pressed the pause button on the movie that they were viewing.

"Sorry to see you go Lor... but this is us, girl! You know it! I don't know why you gotsta get so moody like ya know?" Lorraina's closest friend, Krista, finally reacted.

"We's gunna miss ya! Hope you finally find what you bin lookin' for, or some other sour party pooper like ya'll... Love ya girl". Krista finished and held out her arms to hug Lorraina in a half fakey, half sincere manner.

Lorraina set the bags down and slowly walked over to the couch, sliding her feet on the shaggy olive green carpet, looking at the floor with each step until she reached Krista.

"I'm sorry, Krista... I need something more than this. I gotta go... thanks for caring. I'll keep in touch." They embraced briefly as the movie began again.

No one else even spoke. Lorraina brushed a few tears off of her face with the back of her hand and scurried back to the retro-brown linoleum floor at the entry to grab up her bags.

"We'll miss you!" one guy friend said in a mocking manner, "Not" and then giggles burst out from many of her roommates and their friends.

Lorraina glanced once more around the mismatched, clashing color schemed apartment soaking in the place that she had lived in for eight years now.

She recalled happier days with Krista and some of the other people she roomed with. Days when they were younger and had less, had to make things from scratch, had to survive the bullies and such.

She recollected times when some of them were creative, because they had to be. She thought about times when they actually talked to one another, days before Utopia.

Vividly, a specific memory came to her mind. The teacher explained that they would be following the newly-passed law, and would all move out of their homes at age 15 and be adults under the training of a chosen care corporation.

If they were 15 years old or older, they would not even go home that day. They would have to follow certain rules and laws, but they would be free from "dictating parents", they were told.

To the youth who were scared about this announcement, they re-iterated that it was the new law to alleviate poverty, homelessness, runaways, behavioral programs and more. "It will help the world become happier and more peaceful" the sentence replayed in Lorraina's mind.

"If you don't want to leave your parents yet... too bad! You don't have a choice. This is the new law and order that will fix our land. You are only afraid because you have been brainwashed and indoctrinated to think otherwise by controlling, selfish, parents who have their own agenda." The video proclaimed from every classroom or meetinghouse across the world.

"This will be for your own good and you will see a brighter, happier world because of it, in the not too distant future. You will not be responsible for your own finances yet. You may never be, actually, as we are finalizing our plans for a new financial plan for all as a part of the new order." The woman in the video continued.

Reflecting back, Lorraina knew that it was not really for her good or for any other youth or families good, that at age 15 she and other youth were placed with "new families". She didn't yet understand or know what the reasoning was behind it all, but she knew she was no better off because of it.

Each "family" was chosen collaboratively by a board made up of school districts, the state children's welfare programs, and other federal officials from the United Coalition of Freedom of the Masses (UCFM) and the Health Care for All on Planet Earth (H-CAPE).

All "new families" were designed specifically to create new "equal" families. In each group they tried to choose one or more youth from various cultures, religions, sexual orientations, various heights, weights, education levels, ages, mental health abilities, etc. with an attempt to create balance, equality, tolerance, unity, exposure, etc.

She thought back on the day that her own "new family" was assigned to her. The list posted on their door was so harsh, non-inviting, non-personal, non-feeling, and very stereotypically was as follows, with labels:

Kade –Wheelchair bound (disabled)
Krista - African American and stubborn
Trenton – Anorexic and sickly
Nisha – Lesbian and OCD
Rudy – Large, egotistical football player
Aryn – Gothic and Wiccan
Frenecia – Transgender and vengeful
Lorraina – Christian and girly
Cornelius – Autism and studious
Jake – Germanic/Norwegian and macho
Miranda – Jewish and shy
Park – Korean and unknown

Not only were assignments in "family" members given, but themes, eras of decorations and furniture were given. All youth facilities must have at least two styles and it was encouraged that everyone be able to express themselves through the house décor. This plan was obviously causing the "homes" to be sort of "equal" or "balanced, but to be a very non-aesthetically pleasing type of eclectic.

The day that they had been told they were never to go home to their birth families... they had also been assigned tasks, projects and partners to complete the assignment with.

Collaborative Clock Creations was the title of the first assignment and project. Krista and Lorraina had been paired together and given the task, shortly after being told they would now be sisters in their "new family".

Nerves were bubbling over as they walked toward one another, collecting their instructions and began selecting elements to incorporate into their Collaborative Clock.

It's not that they were nervous about being partners for a class project. They already knew each other a little and were rapidly becoming friends. The news of moving away from their birth families and everything changing so drastically was paralyzing and just shy of debilitating.

Both young ladies were in shock, these things had been talked about, protested, pushed, the center of media attention for years now, but it all seemed distant and surreal when it was just in the news. Never did either of them believe the law would ever finally pass.

They were not the teens who wanted the law to pass necessarily. They were certainly not the teenagers who were rioting in the streets and protesting and fighting to get this new way of life made into law.

Lorraina was afraid of getting hurt or bullied now that she had no parents and family to protect her. Krista was used to being on her own, but she was apprehensive about this new change and the unknown circumstances that she would face.

"There will be no going back home today after school. You will report to your teacher and they will give you instructions where you will be transported via bus to your new locations or homes". The mechanical, computer-sounding, woman's voice on the digital directions interrupted Lorraina's memories of Krista again.

"Your personal belongings will be collected by a security agent and will be gone through to ensure safety and to be sterilized to eliminate germs and potential illnesses. All precious items and heirlooms will be stored for you to collect at your time of departure upon graduation to adulthood" the flashes of that day continued intruding.

"Everything else will then be returned to you at your new residence within the week. Do not be concerned about being cared for – as your new residence boasts all the amenities, toiletries, food and needs you could have. These things will be provided for you free of charge." The voice had broadcast earlier that day.

"Do not report to school here tomorrow as all new schools have been completed just in time for your new stay and living arrangements at this history in the making, ground-breaking, world-wide Order of Utopia" she shuddered at the recollection.

"No one will need to drive or worry about how to get to school, as the new transit system, Omnitrex, has just begun operation today.

"It will take you anywhere you need to go. The loop goes from homes to schools, to stores and to entertainment. Everything is free of charge." Lorraina called to mind nearly in a trance as she had been that fateful day.

Recollecting the moment she broke from that trance, when Krista had interrupted her thoughts with an elbow nudge, Lorraina was back in time still, in her thoughts.

"Hey Lor, you in there?" Krista had raised her voice a little, shaking Lorraina's shoulder after having already nudged her with no response.

"I'm sorry, I'm just in shock." Lorraina whispered to her friend. "Does this mean that we never get to say goodbye to our families? What about our siblings. Will they get to be in our new families with us, when they are old enough? I'm so confused and scared" Lorraina continued whispering.

"A pain is in my heart and an ache in my soul like I've never experienced. I feel like I was just in a terrible accident and my entire family died." Lorraina whispered loud enough now that the teacher cleared his throat and reminded all students to stop talking, stay focused and work on their clocks.

"At least I get to be with you" Lorraina finished barely audibly as soon as the teacher looked away.

"Oooh, look at these pretty silver bubbles" Krista said as they sorted through the options for their new clock, a symbol of starting time anew, making a change, and time starting over with the creation of their new clocks on this first day of anew order and new law and life because of it.

"I love bubbles too, and those are really pretty!" Lorraina responded sadly, attempting to move on and distract herself. "I don't mind if we make a bubble themed clock. The rules do say we have to combine two themes together though. So let's find something that goes well with silver bubbles for a second theme."

Sauntering throughout the room, slipping between tables, desks, chairs, and counters of their soon to be "old" classroom, both girls took their time. Not only were they looking at the items provided for the clock project ... but they soaked in the musty aroma of the room, the slight breeze through the window, the heat of the day, the flies buzzing, the new paint smell where the maintenance crew tried to cover and seal old chipping paint.

Shelved in memories, the normalcy of it all soaked into their beings, fearfully wondering how it would all be when they left that school and everything they'd known before, moments after the bell rang.

"I found it!!!" Krista interjected, having come across something... and then shouted out, "Something that goes well with SILVER bubble shapes" hiding the item behind her back suspiciously.

Looking at Krista with slight uncertainty, Lorraina was awaiting the item with a questioning look, head tilted close to her right shoulder and one eyebrow raised. Lorraina had caught on to the facetious tone in Krista's voice, but didn't know whether the sarcasm was about her, the teacher, or any random soul, as Krista was a very jaded and cynical person.

"Golden bubbles!" Krista exclaimed loudly, giggling so intensely that the teacher darted another stern look, and shushed them. They tried to be quiet, but desperately needed to laugh, so they could refrain from crying at such a painful, indeterminate time. They ceased their laughing regardless, as the teacher walked over to them sternly, approaching and glaring harshly at the two of them.

"You're walking on thin ice girls! I'm about to have you separated... Do you want that?"

"No sir" They both said respectfully in unison.

"Then I'd advise you to be quiet and get to work, NOW!" Mr. Devon roared.

Krista and Lorraina went directly to focusing quietly on their assignment and continued keeping quiet, their heads down, out of fear, until the clock was complete.

Two hours later they still awaited their clock to be graded in the "final judgment" of their project. Also for their teacher to ensure that they followed all of the rules.

They were a bit fidgety with extreme nerves, and all they could think about was how rude and bossy their teacher was and would they pass his class? Would it matter? Would they start school as freshman all over again? Would they pick up where they left off or start all over? etc.

Reaching the last of their immature patience, Mr. Devon finally walked over to their homemade clock. He looked at the fine workmanship and cohesiveness of it all and ran his fingers across it, realizing it was top quality and looked as if it was store bought.

No one else's did. He stopped briefly and looked at the floor. He didn't speak a word, only a sound of disgust, as he placed an F sticker right on the face of the clock and walked away.

"Why?!" Krista yelled out to him.

"It's beautiful and well done" Lorraina said in a quieter tone, but still questioning. The other students either had left the classroom with their clocks, or were leaving.

Mr. Devon began to explain, "It only had one theme, you were supposed to learn to work together and be tolerant."

"But she chose silver and I chose gold Mr. Devon." Lorraina plead.

"I don't want to hear another word, and since you failed the final (this was the final by the way), you fail the class" he barked. "Oh, and remember girls, you may not like it, but you have no parents to go whine to now and save the day!"

After briefly pausing, he gruffly continued, "In fact, while I still have you in my classroom, before you move on to Mr. Howard tomorrow, you can now both clean up the classroom. You can..." Mr. Devon was interrupted by the bell.

"Looks like that's our cue, to be free of you!" Krista blurted in a sassy rhyming tone. "Since you aint our teacha' no mo', we aint gotsta listen to ya no mo'!" she finished snatching up the clock and clutching Lorraina's arm headed out.

Just as she reached the door, she turned and finished, "And by the way Mr. Devon, we aint got parents no mo', but we's adults now, ya hear! So no mo' talking down to us, ya hear?!" and she pushed Lorraina through the doorway, walked out with her head held high and slammed the door.

Lorraina came back from her flashes and memories of the past and realized that still no one was paying any attention. She cleared the lump in her throat and opened the door quietly. She walked out and closed it. Closing the door not only to her house, but to that chapter in her life, she couldn't help but focus her attention on the plaque on the door.

"#2719, Of the Order of Utopia" it read. Under that it read "The Promise of Tolerance and Peace".

"Sickening!" Lorraina blurted out loud and turned her back on the door and the sign. She set her bags down, took a deep breath, and bowed her head. "Please God, help me in this endeavor, help me find my family, and help me forgive." She picked her bags up, and made her way to the housing headquarters to pick up personal belongings and check out.

CHAPTER 3

The walk was very long, but there was no other way. There were no cars on the premises and the Omnitrex rail did not stop at the housing office. Finally arriving, Lorraina was out of breath, and a little sweaty in her jacket.

She had been wearing it so that she didn't have to carry it. She didn't have enough room in her bags, but it was 70*F, the sun was radiating down upon her, and the air stale and stagnant. "Excuse me" Lorraina said into the intercom as she held down the red button, "I need to check out."

"All people who leave the premises must check out. They may only be away for 2 hours and then must check back in" a women's voice read methodically over a loud buzzing speaker. "If anyone is to be out any longer, they must check out permanently and NEVER return. They have paperwork to complete too" the woman said now glancing up from her reading, looking through the top of her glasses.

"Why do you want to leave again, Lorraina?" She protested with her tone of voice, obviously recognizing Lorraina.

"Trying to find your parents again?" said the older woman's voice on the other side of the glass through the intercom.

"Yes, ma'am!"

"You've already checked out 5 times and haven't found them...What's going to be different this time?"

"I'll go farther than a 2 hour radius this time" Lorraina said excitedly through the intercom. The woman buzzed the office door open and Lorraina went into an entry waiting area that also still had glass, but was easier to speak through with no button to hold and at least some air conditioning.

"You're not allowed to leave for longer than 2 hours, Lorraina", the woman responded emphatically through the bullet proof glass. "You know you're not allowed to."

"You said if I checked out permanently I could." Lorraina responded innocently and naïvely, more like a child than the adult that she had now been for a while.

"Permanently?!?!" The woman's voice was raised and she became aggressive, irritated, and authoritative. "Why would you want to do that? Everything is free here and great and clean and perfect... well, close to anyways. Besides, this helps with everyone seeing our example of tolerance and peace."

The woman's heavy coat of hairspray, makeup and body mist were leaching a strong aroma of perfume even through the intercom as she continued. "You are a selfish girl, Lorraina! We certainly needed and still need more acceptance and tolerance in our world. Can't you see that things are going very well?"

Taking a formal, professional breather including a sip of water and smoothing her fall-toned scarf to control her reactions, the woman continued. "Everyone is learning to become so much more tolerant and our world is so much more peaceful, Lorraina. Just think about that before making such a huge life-changing decision that will affect you and others" she faked caring.

"Tolerant?!? Peaceful?!? Have you subjected yourself to one of these "family" experiments?" Lorraina finally, for one of the few times in her life, began to lose her temper.

"You have no idea of what you speak! Was it 'tolerance' when my first day in my new family Jake held me down while Rudy raped me as I was begging for my new 'brothers' to please not touch me? Was it 'peaceful' when Jake then took a turn?"

Lorraina took a deep breath and tried to calm herself down a bit, but was unable to. "I guess it was 'tolerance' when I had to hear Krista and the other girls and one of the guys get raped too, as I was tied up and could do nothing to stop it".

"Calm down Lorraina, You know..." The clerk was cut off by Lorraina.

"I suppose you'd like to call it 'tolerance' when every day thereafter and sometimes multiple times a day I, or my roommates, got raped by other 'family members' too. Or should I call it incest since they were supposed to be my family?" embarrassed and red-faced Lorraina was exhibiting remarkable restraint for her "blow-up".

"Well I guess I did 'tolerate' it" Lorraina slowed down a little, "because if I fought, begged, cried or showed any emotion, Rudy hurt me more and did it more often or was meaner during the act".

"So," she went on solemnly. "I showed nothing and became dead inside and to the world. I held everything in, having no joy, just tolerating my 'new life' until he got bored and moved out and on to other things when he turned 18. So did we all become dead! We survived mostly by watching movies and getting our brains distracted."

Glancing down at the floor she proceeded, "I guess that was your version of 'tolerance' and accepting your horrific 'new world' of whoever's the biggest, meanest and strongest wins... But let me ask you, if you had undergone this 'tolerance' for the last few years – would you still call this 'social experiment' peaceful?" Lorraina concluded, darting her gaze up toward the secretary, questioning her with her eyes.

"Well, it is just that – an experiment" the woman answered without hesitation in a callous manner. "It notifies everyone in the program description and bylaws that we cannot determine or foresee the outcome. It is with great confidence, however, that we believe this new Order of Utopia will be in the best collective interest of all".

"Miss Fenton, how can you stand there and be so..." Lorraina was cut short this time by the secretary.

"Maybe you were just asking for it, young lady" Miss Fenton snarked, egotistically and with considerable lack of feeling. "Now, either way, your stuff is not accessible right now and it's past 5:00, so we are closed."

The clerk finished in a hostile way as she walked out and around and firmly pulled down the metal scroll down door, in an irritated manner. Miss Fenton turned away from Lorraina not responding at all and walked back into the reception office; heels clicking behind her, her presence now vanished from Lorraina's sight.

Having no indication what to do now, Lorraina exited the building and just sat on a cement bench near the grassy area in front of the main housing office. Everything in her made her desire to just leave and not worry about checking out, but she would get some kind of fee or bill or ticket or something and she was pretty sure that she couldn't make it out of the gates as there were guards keeping watch and security systems.

She knew of bills and tickets and such things that her parents used to deal with, and she was aware that they at least had existed before the Order of Utopia. She wasn't sure what it would be like now, or was like on the outside. Also, she wanted her heirlooms and personal effects that had been held for safe keeping, so she stayed.

"What should I do though?" She wondered out loud to herself. "I can't go back now," she mumbled. She felt that would be far too humiliating and she really wanted to be out of there. Determining that she couldn't even consider going back, she decided to camp out with her bags on the thin strip of lawn in front of the headquarters until morning.

There were large walls and gates 20' tall all around the community and security guards not only watching the gate, but vigilantly patrolling the perimeter. There was no way in or out, without permission. She'd observed some of her peers attempting to escape, and getting caught and punished severely, or even disappearing. There were also cameras everywhere outside, so she knew she would be on camera and hoped she would be safe – just as much as in the home she'd just fled, behind Utopia door #2719.

There wasn't much Lorraina could do to stay warm enough later that evening. The climate in the area was hot and dry during the days. This having left Lorraina parched and drenched in sweat simultaneously during the sunlight – and now she was still parched and beginning to shiver, due to her clothes still being damp with her sweat.

Even with the above average heat wave they'd been experiencing in December during the days, rapidly upon the setting of the sun, the heat fled the soil and beige stucco walls of the buildings. Temperatures dropped typically to somewhere between 35 – 50 degrees Fahrenheit at night, and piercing cold began gripping at Lorraina as the remaining light seemed to hastily take flight.

Lamp posts and street lights sputtered on and Lorraina could feel the opposite of warmth, penetrating her skin long before she finally got out her cell phone and checked to see that it was a bitter 39 degrees.

Wrapping herself in her sleeping bag, she'd carried with her luggage earlier that day, after dressing in three layers and a jacket... Lorraina still felt the stinging cold through it all.

As Lorraina lay on the grass with one suitcase bag under her head and upper back, another underneath right arm, she balled up her body to keep heated as much as she could during such a vicious darkness. She wondered if her siblings ever had to suffer this way. "What about my parents?" she pondered.

"Oh, I can't wait to find them. I wonder what my siblings will look like now" she whispered and chatted to herself to try and distract from the pain her toes and fingertips were beginning to feel. "Greg would be 28 by now, Rebekah age 19, Alec age 16, Frederick age 13, and Jillian age 9. I can't even imagine most of their faces" she chattered on in a mumbly, grumbly sort of way.

"Jillian was only one year old, just a baby, when I last saw her" she continued speaking out loud in order to not feel afraid of the dark. "Did mom have anymore? Is Greg married yet? Are Rebekah and Alec in another facility like this one? Are there other facilities?" Lorraina began to rock a little to attempt to keep warm.

She'd looked for her siblings and she watched constantly for any of them. While Utopia was excessively large, she hadn't seen them. She may have missed them, she hoped not. "Oh, I hope not" she mumbled shivering and rocking.

The night stretched on agonizingly as Lorraina kept dosing off momentarily. She was trying to stay awake, to make sure she wouldn't fall asleep forever, due to the crisp temperature. Looking at her device every 15-20 minutes or so though, she finally realized she'd almost made it through the night. The sun would be coming up any moment.

As the sun began to come up and warm the earth and her life.... So did the sprinklers. Dashing away from the water and grasping her things and getting them away from the water – was not quick enough.

She was drenched and so were the three layers of clothes that she was wearing and some of her bags. The temptation to just go home was real and intense, but she didn't want to go home or start over, she needed to get out now while she still could. Determined to see her family again one day, she was absolutely not interested in going back.

Wringing out her jacket and backpack still dressed in multiple layers, the first employee showed up for work for the day. It was an elderly man with a navy blue jumpsuit and an ID number in red lettering that read, UTOPIA3535933.

He was quiet and solemn and Lorraina hadn't seen any person older than 30 in the facility other than the lady she'd just been talking to. She couldn't help but stare a little, but then neither could he. He was attempting to rationalize and figure out in his head why she wanted to goof off in the water so early in the morning when it was still so chili.

"You are soaking wet" the old man stated after a long silence.

"Yes, I know!" she responded shortly, feeling rather annoyed. "I got soaked from the sprinkler system. Is there a place that I could go to, to change clothes?" she questioned.

He held his hand and arm out pointing the direction with his hand, never saying a word, after his first statement. After motioning the way, as Lorraina walked, he followed. She was a tad uneasy now, but felt that there was no choice, and he seemed kind enough.

Continuing, he utilized his arm to signal her on, until they reached a private room – the old man lead on in silence. He motioned for her to go in. As she stepped in, after he unlocked the door, he quickly stepped in too.

Now she was terrified. "What did I get myself into?" she said out loud. "Please don't hurt me, please don't hurt me!!!" She frantically cried covering her face, having dropped her bags to the floor.

"Shhh... no stop it, listen... just listen... I'm not going to hurt you, or do anything to you. I'm trying to talk to you!" he said with his hands up to show her he was unarmed and not trying to hurt her.

"Please listen" he continued, "You don't have much time" he insisted quietly. She backed up and calmed down a bit, trying to listen, now that she felt less threatened.

"I know I will lose my job for this, and likely lose my life for this." He began.

"For what?"

"Trying to help you! You should not have been here. I brought you to this room because it is the only room that is not recorded. There are no cameras in here. It is the private suite of Mr. Avera. He is the designer of Utopia. He doesn't live here, he just visits – thank goodness, but every place else in Utopia is recorded and under surveillance."

"What? Why?' Lorraina asked in a fearful whisper. "I don't understand, you mean they had cameras in our houses and our rooms?"

"Everywhere, but the bathrooms, and even of that I am not 100% sure that they were not recording or watching."

"What?" Lorraina gasped pulling away and walking back a step almost falling over. Horrified, as she flashed through all of her memories of rape, clothes changing, and hundreds or even thousands of unwanted footage of herself being recorded and possibly stored somewhere, she nearly threw up in disgust. "Isn't that illegal?" she demanded.

"Not in Utopia! You see Mr. Avera and his creeps make all the laws and rules. Unfortunately, kid, the only way for you to get out of here alive right now, is to listen to me and follow my directions. They always check the footage at 4:00 pm, unless there was a problem or something amiss".

He paused briefly looking around for cameras and being further guarded. "They're going to notice that something was amiss, so you are going to have to distract, by staying soaking wet, yelling, demanding and insisting that you leave. I have seen how this works, those who go quietly most often disappear (like get killed or "X-d" they call it). Those who throw a fit, they give a bill and the law on the other side makes them pay the bill. If they don't, they get X-d. If they do, but they talk about things from here... from this side too much, they get X-d too."

Lorraina was squinting as she was attempting to see through streaks of water streaming down her face from her wet hair on top of her head. The older worker was no less quick, hardworking, and light on his feet than any average younger man. He noticed this issue and swiftly darted to the bathroom and came back with a hand-towel and tossed it at Lorraina and then went back to explaining.

"They X people by claiming they were not vaccinated and died of a disease, or saying they killed themselves or a relative killed them or now they are in an institution etc. Always some lie of how they died. But not true, never believe them.

"Miss Fenton, the head of this department," he continued. "Is very callous and crooked, she hopes to convince Mr. Avera to notice her and share in his wealth somehow, she is enamored with him, and of course he doesn't like her, but uses this to his advantage to keep loyal, patriotic employees who nearly worship him".

"Anyhow" he began to speak more rapidly and intensely. "She is going to be in rather shortly, so we gotta get you outside soon. Just, ask her for whatever you were going to ask her, but be demanding and loud and annoying and she'll let you out."

"Then what?" Lorraina questioned.

"I don't know, I haven't gotten that far. Be smart, alert and savvy; go as far from here as you can once they let you out. Don't report where they tell you to.

They are often in cahoots with the police and military on the other side."

"How do you know all of this?"

"That's a story for another time, but let me just say... I bury the bodies and clean up their messes... I am not proud of that and I haven't killed anyone myself, but I don't want to be burying you later".

"Will I see you again? I just don't know my way around out there".

"Unfortunately yes... Either we're going to die together once they watch this footage, or we're going to escape together."

"I don't understand."

"We don't have time to talk about it. There's three minutes til the hour and Miss Fenton is usually right on time. I come early or she yells at me. Anyway, all I can say is when you get out, head east, go two miles, and when you see the sign for Sewage Treatment Facility... head there. They do not keep that monitored or guarded all the time, and there are some large tanks to hide behind".

"Tanks? What kind of tanks?" Lorraina was now feeling even more uncertain and afraid.

"Just wait there, and I will try and meet you. If not... well, wait there anyway. I may be dead, but they'll be looking for you. They won't imagine a spoiled kid from here would go there... Now, get" he said, opening the door and nudging her forward.

As they sped up their pace through the halls, almost slipping on the water that Lorraina was dripping off of herself – they rounded a corner and came near a bathroom. They could hear a voice, Miss Fenton's voice. Grumbling and calling for him, "Richard!" she hollered.

"Just coming" he said grabbing the wet sleeve on Lorraina's shoulder as you would a prisoner. As Miss Fenton rounded the corner, she gasped.

"What is all this?" she asked angrily.

"This is the riffraff I found playing in my sprinklers this morning" he replied, trying to make things up in his mind to say, as he went along.

"Not sure what she was up to, but I hauled her in here and was just telling her to clean up, when you came around the corner."

"Well!" Miss Fenton glared at Lorraina, grabbed her shoulder, turned her around and marched her into the bathroom. "You mop up this mess, Richard," she bellowed, "We can't have any lawsuits."

"Right, yes ma'am." Richard bowed and agreed, lowering his head and acting as a slave, very humbly and groveling like. He quickly mopped up the area that lead to Mr. Avera's quarters and handled that first, and ran back to handle the rest.

Meanwhile, in the bathroom, Miss Fenton shoved Lorraina forward a little. "What do you think you're doing? Who do you think you are?" she demanded.

"I don't think I'm anybody, I just want to check out and I want my keepsakes. I slept on the lawn and almost froze to death." Lorraina hollered, remembering Richard's advice. "And then I was accosted by a sprinkler system this morning. That guy saw me, grabbed me by the back of my shirt and dragged me in here. He scared the daylights out of me and told me to clean up. I just want my personal effects and to go." Lorraina insisted, folding her arms in irritation.

"Unfortunately, I guess we failed to announce or inform you that the room that housed everyone's personal effects, had a major fire three months ago. Everything, and I mean everything... burned to the ground. You have nothing!"

"Nothing?!?!" Lorraina hollered back in the woman's face. "Nothing?!?!" she repeated, knowing that this wasn't the truth, as she had been to this office every month for the last three months, trying to get up enough courage to check out of the facility for good.

There had been no fire damage and no construction or anything out of place that would indicate that the building had had any problems at all, let alone a fire that burned everything.

Lorraina realized that she was not going to get her personal effects now, regardless of whatever the lie, even if they really did have them. So, she became selective suddenly with her words and tried not to show any body gestures. She was now very guarded and could see that Richard was right.

"Not even my photos, or my parent's special keepsakes that they dropped off for me? I can't even believe that this is happening to me." She raised her voice, now definitely crying at the thought of losing the only bit of her family she had, til she could hopefully find them and reunite one day.

Even if the true cause of why she lost these items, was a lie. "Please" Lorraina began again. "Don't you have any records of where my parents might be? Do you think that I will ever find them?"

"Certainly not, young lady! Your parents could even be dead by now, it's a rough life out there" Miss Fenton retorted briskly.

Rapidly racing, Lorraina's mind was thoroughly attempting to figure out a way out of this predicament. Remembering Richard's words of advice to be loud and obnoxious, Lorraina came up with a solution.

"Ahhhhhhhh, waa haha waaaaaaaa, waswaswas, uh huh u hu" Lorraina whined and wailed and made strange unrecognizable sounds and noises with snorts and coughs in between them.

"Plea he heeee heeee heeees" Lorraina continued. "Please will you be my new mommy and adopt me then?" And then the crazy mutated sounds and whines continued in an excruciatingly annoying manner.

"Wa ha ha ha ha, uh hu, eee ahhh, orrr ha ho huh u wa wa awwe.."

"Stop it! Just stop it right now!" screamed Miss Fenton, demanding Lorraina stop as she pounded on the bathroom counter between the sinks.

Lorraina only slowed for seconds and then became more intense. "Eeeeeeeeeeeee Errrrrrrrrrppppppp wahahahahaaaaaaa, ggnooooort snnaaaaaa haaaa haaaz baaaa!"

"Shut up!" Miss Fenton screeched again at maximum decibels for her voice box. "No!!!

I will never be your mother, nor will I have any children. What is freaking wrong with you?" She demanded as Lorraina continued and then began drooling heavily very near Miss Fenton's high-heels.

"Wahhhhhhh Uuuuuuuuuhhhhh, huhuhu ororororor! Buuu huuut liiiiii ha hihihi neeeeeeeeeeed to stay until you can leaaaaaaarn learrr haaa huuuurrrnnnn hurnnn to Luuuuuuuuvvvvvvvvv" Lorraina was stopped pre-maturely by Miss Fenton.

"Somebody get her out of my sight now!" she hollered into her intercom, turning her back on Lorraina and walking out of the bathroom into the hall.

"Richard, keep an eye on this girl now!" She snapped quickly and began walking away from him back to the office. "Will you get her off of our premises and checked out forever... She's demented".

Richard could hear her fading in the distance on the microphone, but also on his own, as the shrieking and donkey noises were continuing from the bathroom.

CHAPTER 4

Shortly after, Lorraina and her bags were thrown out of the gates and the gates began to shut.

"I don't know where I'm going, I need help. I want back in, I have no family left. Miss Fenton said she'd adopt me," the 23 year-old insisted.

"Oh my gosh! You are going to be the death of me, woman!" one of the guards yelled. "Hey Richard, you love to be worthless and help people. Why don't you help this deranged girl to get the heck out of here ASAP? And help us never see her again. We'll give you a chance with this one. Use whatever force necessary to silence her." The guard said, clearing his throat in a knowing manner.

"You mean...?" Richard asked.

"Whatever is necessary" he said, opening the gate and shoving Richard out.

"But what about my hours for today?" Richard beat on the gates.

"We'll leave you clocked in, ha ha ha" they were laughing now. "However long it takes to dispose of her, it's fine with us, it's on the clock. We don't want her and it's about time you took a turn. Just do it Richard! Get rid of her, haha. Stupid piece of annoying trash!"

Richard turned, his fortune had turned too. Actually, his whole life had turned. He knew once they watched the footage at 4pm... he was toast. At least it gave him a head start. Richard just began walking, not saying a word. Lorraina got scared and chased after. He went at a slow, calm, steady pace until the guards were out of site.

CHAPTER 5

The door shut and a quiet jingling of an eclectic door chime with small shells and bell-like ornaments was audible in the small, cozy shop near the coastline of a little town in Washington State.

"Can I help you, young man?" a woman said in a deep rich tone, full of a sincere desire to help people. This young man was 11 years of age, and a tad small for his age. He was wiry with big thick turtle shell toned, plastic glasses frames, a wavy mop of dirty blonde, curly hair, and with gnarly teeth.

He had passed by the shop many times, eying the items from the outside through the display window. Often he'd go pacing back and forth, trying to get up the courage to enter, yet instead finally dashing off.

Gone for a week or so, he would then finally return, tattered and messy as usual, yet with curious, longing gazes through the glass storefront window. The store owner and caretaker felt as if she almost knew him; she'd watched him gawking at the items so very many times.

"I have a lot of items in here" she began again, pausing ever so briefly. "Many of them are very inexpensive or cheap and I have a sale today. It's 50% off for the next hour." She waited a bit longer this time, watching the boy wander about quietly, scarcely even looking up.

He was twisting his hands together, pulling at his individual fingers, and shuffling his feet. He was then dragging them heavily against the weathered beach style, white washed, boardwalk-type flooring inside. He was mulling over what he might purchase in this store full of unique treasures and valuables to some, considered trash and junky memorabilia – quite possibly – to others.

"Hey son, how old are you?" A pleasant voice again interrupted the hush in the coastal shop.

The boy's head darted up. "I'm not supposed to tell strangers things like that!" he snapped a little.

"Ok, you are right, I'm sorry."

He continued to nervously drag his way around all the clothes racks, bins, and baskets of small rocks and shells. Flip flops – some of them mismatched and some of them even home woven or home decorated with beads, shells, or other ocean themed styles, were arranged all throughout the seaside gift-shop.

"This bin is free?!?!" The boy exclaimed in an inquisitive manner.

"Yes, it is free!" The storekeeper warmly and lovingly responded as if the young child were her own son. "Please feel free to rummage through it and pick anything you like out of it, and take it home with you."

"Why is it free? Is there a catch?" the young man started. "My dad told me nothing in this world is free, and that if it is advertised as so, it is a trick or a downright lie."

"Well, the answer to that question comes in three parts. So if you want to really know if it's free, you need to listen to the entire answer without talking".

Giving the boy no time to respond, she began, "You see, my father always taught me that you need to listen so that you could hear and understand. You should try to imagine yourself in the speaker's shoes, and even if you disagree with them, you should find some way to show that you care".

She went on, without hardly even a break or breath, glad someone was listening to her. "We should never listen to others just to find a way to shut them up, win an argument, or just to respond... and he told me that even sometimes we have to let people be wrong – if it isn't endangering anybody - because anytime we fight, solely to prove we are right, we are in the wrong".

"Ma'am, I'm willing to listen, and I'm not trying to fight... but I really don't understand you! I didn't understand what you were saying to me."

Breathing a sigh of exhaustion and frustration, she realized that she was talking way above his level of understanding. She tried to restate her words at a level more suited for children.

"So, what I'm trying to say is that we need to be more kind and caring about others and as I told one of my friends one time, I'm going to write a new book called, *Don't Judge Another Mother Until You've Danced in Her Glass Slippers*, do you understand now?"

"You are a writer!" the boy said excitedly.

"Ummm... no... nope. I'm not yet, that's not what I meant. I mean I want to be a writer and I am working on a book, but actually what I was trying to say..." she paused catching her breath. "Is that a lot of people like to judge others, and they are very rude and totally hypocritical and they laugh about it and they're not even funny, and they need to work on walking a mile in other people's shoes. Hence the analogy of the shoes, and well - glass slippers, which were Cinderella's shoes and people judged her when she was poor and had worn out shoes. And when she had glass slippers and then lost one, they judged her too. So I'm not entirely sure whether I will name it with slippers, or slipper, singular."

"Do you have any kids?" the boy asked chopping her off a little abruptly.

"No... why do you ask?" she responded.

"Cuz, you're not making a lot of sense and I was wondering how your kids can understand all of this."

"I guess I'm just nervous and bored. I don't get a lot of people in here. Sorry! Did you understand anything that I was trying to say?"

"I think that you're saying that you really like shoes, and that's why you make them and sell them in this bin in your shop. But you wish you had glass slippers like Cinderella, so that's why you're going to write a book about it... because there's no real fairy godmother. That part I do know for sure!"

"Oh boy, kiddo, you should be a shrink. I've never realized the things you just said about liking shoes and wishing for a happier life. Dang, you got me pegged!"

"Well, I don't know anything about being pegged. I'm already small enough, so I don't need to shrink, but I do know that my dad always says that all women like shoes and wish for more stuff, so I guess you're not that different."

"WOW! Sounds like your daddy is pretty sure about things and has had a very difficult life that makes him a little grumpy?!" she said, half inquiring.

"Oh, no, ma'am, not a little grumpy, he's a lot grumpy, all the time! He loves to yell and hit and get his anger out by breaking stuff. He could never come into this store; he'd ruin all of it. Then I would have no special place to dream about anymore."

"What's your name, hon?" she asked again, a little concerned for the lad, hoping he wasn't getting beaten, and wanting to make sure that he actually had a parent.

"My daddy taught me never to tell people my name, but I guess he never said you couldn't tell people your nickname. My nickname is Liam, its short for William. I better go now, though... Oh yah, what's your name?" he said, beginning to head towards the door to exit.

"Bridge, my nickname is Bridge, its short for Bridget."

"Wow, I've never heard of such a name for a person, only for a bridge that cars go on. That's cool! I'll always remember that."

"Ok and I'll remember yours. I can't wait to see you again in a few weeks – or sooner – and then I'll tell you why I have a free bin, but if you want, there are no strings attached and I would love for you to have something out of the free bin now."

"I think I'd better wait till I have time to hear the whole story, because my dad said that even though Pinocchio didn't have real strings, the bad guys tricked him and the other boys and the invisible strings made them turn into donkeys. I'm not falling for 'invisible strings'! My dad says that FREE stuff always has invisible strings." Liam paused at the door and then half-turned back towards Bridget.

"But thank you! Have a good day!" He quickly disappeared off toward the hills and she watched him till he vanished out of sight.

CHAPTER 6

"What in the heck is wrong with you boy?" Mr. Heepen bellowed in a hostile manner. "You some kind of freakin' mutant troll or something? You like the trolls my folks done tell me legends about in Alaska. Those stick men or whatever they called 'em. They live under ground and appear from behind rocks in the forest outta nowhere, ya know?!?"

"Daddy you been drink'n too much again. Please... remember the doctor told ya you'd go n' have a stroke if you keep on drinkin'." Liam quietly pleaded with his father.

"Daddy?!? Daddy?!? Ain't you too old to be callin' me daddy no mo'?" Mr Heepen mockingly mimicked his son.

"I'm sorry sir, I won't call you that anymore. I'm sorry Dad, only please just remember your blood levels. Both the blood pressure and the sugars, remember? Please, just go rest, so nothing happens. Please, dad!" Liam continued his appeal to his aggressive, inebriated father.

"So that nothing happens?!? Nothing happens!!! What you'd expect to happen?" Howard Heepen again attempted to copy his son in a degrading, hurtful, broken English, uneducated, and uncaring way.

"I didn't mean that, I meant so that nothing happens to you pa. Please pa, I just am worried about you, pa!"

"Pa? Dad? Daddy?" Howard Heepen altered his voice into a creepy, mousy version of what he impersonated his son to sound like. "I'm done with all those, I'm done with you! I'm done raising you. I'm done with you tellin' me what to do. You just like ya stupid ma. Always wantin' mo', tryin' to stop me from my potential" his voice slurred and gagged a bit as he spoke, making no logical sense.

"Ok. Dad please, I get so scared when you get like this."

"Like what, boy? Like what? Like myself, like a man, like a strong man in control of his own life? Like a man who's sick of being lied to, mistreated, cheated on, left behind, you name it, boy, and yo' mama done it to me". Howard continued, his voice elevating to higher and higher decibels with every word.

Growling and staggering towards his ever trembling son, Howard's gauntlet of questions continued. "Why'd you think I'm so fulla hate boy? Why you think Yo' mama did this ta me? She made me this, boy. You happy with this, boy?" He motioned to himself as he rhetorically interrogated.

His tone falling to nearly a whisper, he continued, feeble and dizzy momentarily. "You got her ta blame! Only her! Do you see her around here helping out, providing, takin' care of anything? No, course not!" His levels increasing rapidly again. "She ruined me!!!" he screamed as his eyes appeared nearly separated from his face.

Wiping the sweat from his forehead and long straight, grey bangs, he continued: "She stuck me with ya' and runned off to find her dreams and a handsomer, better feller. Never mind that nothing and no one eva' coulda' been good'nuff fo' her" he slurred and spit now as he fluctuated up and down in his volume.

Tripping around the room and into furniture and the like, Howard continued to walk around the room. He was coming towards Liam, as Liam continued to be discreet and not very noticeably move himself slowly about the living area, off the kitchen.

Darting quietly and effectively around the couch in the middle of the room, Liam continued as his father was ever attempting to reach him, not able to think of more than one thing at a time and notice why Liam kept being so far from his grasp, as he followed and bellowed at Liam. "She ruined me, boy! And you are turnin' just like her. That makes me hate you! I hate that you remind me of her and that you is doing this to me. You hear me son? You hear me boy?"

No answer would have satisfied the man, so Liam intentionally remained silent, due to personal past experiences. Any answer that he could have given his father would have incited him even further.

Even his silence could not keep Mr. Heepen from releasing his anger at that point. "I mean like I said kid, you ain't my son!!! No son of mine would pretend to know better than his pa. No son of mine would be tellin' his dad what ta do!" The roaring had intensified again.

Howard leaned back a little and up against the island counter in their kitchen, stabilizing himself. He felt for the fifties-style, red bar stool and slunk back a tad and sat onto it. "In fact," he started slowly, looking at the ground with a bit longer of waits between words this time. "You is old enough now to get out! You's old enough! I was on my own and raisin' my own self when I was gall darn only 7 years old. You already 11, boy. Why should I need to fork out money to feed you, boy?" he stopped speaking and looked up at his son full of anger, pain, and partial revenge. His anger was actually directed at his long-lost wife, but with her long out of the picture, he was fixating it all onto Liam.

"I am your son, Pa!" Liam broke into the drunken, shocking, one-sided conversation as his father had sort of tapered off. "I am your son… and you don't have to fork out money, Pa. Remember that the Utopia school company pays for my meals now even before I am old enough to go there."

Liam was reaching for anything he could think of, to help his plight and convince his father to keep him.

"Remember I saw the sign at school that said 'New Utopia Meal Deals for financially effected families'. Remember I brought you the papers, you filled it out and we've been getting a daily box that I pick up for us every day?"

"I remember, you punk. If you didn't see that dumb poster I'd still have my guns and I coulda' killed you, me, or us both by now and gotten us outta' this rotten world." He paused, hanging his head low, resting his forehead into one hand with a bottle of alcohol in the other.

A wave of guilt swept across Mr. Heepen's expression as he looked up wide-eyed with not even a blink. Even through his level of intoxication, he hesitated on his words, ever so briefly, but still wrestling and throwing off his better inner-half. "One of us goes today! I can't take lookin' at you no mo'! You stinkin' look so much like your ma and I hate that you also look like him, and you ruin it for me". He stood up and escalated again, kicking away his last bit of conscience.

"Him? Who are you talking about dad?" Liam's face grew contorted with worry, confusion, and fear as he held back his tears.

"Every gall darn day, I gotta remember my pain and hurt and that she done this to me and I can't let go of the hate. Your older brothers have already all long gone. That Utopia place says it'll take folks like you!"

"Pa, what are you talking about? What do you mean I look like him? Who are you talking about? Pa, I look like you. We have the same crooked teeth and nose and the same curled ear. I don't under..."

"Utopia says it'll take kids 10 and up if the parents can't handle them, if the kid is troubled, a runaway, has behavioral problems, or if the parent just doesn't want them anymore"

"No, Dad!!! No, you don't know what happens in there! You don't know what they do!" Liam's own voice was raising and stirring with panic and pleading. He now spoke, more fearful of the unknown than the beating he might get, or the broken glass shards or items he may have to clean up.

"But Dad," he became unrelenting. "Remember we've never heard from the boys since they left? Remember, we don't even get letters or cards. Pa, you can't be serious?! Please Dad, please... I want to be here with you! I've got no one else. Ma already left us, she left me too, not just you".

Frantically intensifying, Liam groveled, "I lost the brothers, my older brothers. I lost mom! You can't turn your back on me and take me to that awful place... you can't!!! Please dad! Please! I am begging you... I love you!

"No Liam! You're not even mine!"

"I want to be able to call you or write to you..." Liam just raced his words right over Howard's. "Please... I don't want to never hear from you again and only when I'm 11. Please dad, please." Liam sobbed and entreated as Howard swigged and then gulped hard, more alcohol to kill his conscience. "Please, I don't know what else you even want from me. I've tried so hard!"

Howard Heepen looked cold suddenly. He grabbed the large bottle of hard liquor at the neck of the bottle tighter and tighter. He lifted it to the sky and said "a toast to truth and free tomorrows."

Then, keeping his eyes fixed on Liam he put the bottle to the side of his head and leaned back sideways to chug down the remainder of the 'bad juice' as Liam called it, still staring widely at Liam.

Down, he smashed the bottle onto an elegant table, passed on to him from his family since the early 1900s. The table – being one of the only nice things left in the room – Howard had to put a dent in the last thing Liam had always tried to protect, when his father was sloshed.

As the glass shards shattered everywhere and cut his hand, Howard continued holding his hand up toward

Liam. "This blood is not your blood! My blood doesn't flow through your veins. I'm not your dad. I may have taken you in all these years, but your mama cheated on me! She cheated!!! I hate her every day for it."

Wincing with pain and now grabbing a cloth out of an overstuffed drawer that wasn't shut all of the way, Howard continued to speak. "I stayed during the pregnancy. I dealt with it all. I was mean and cold to her durin' the whole 9 months, but I still stayed. I did my duty and more. I fed her and you. That's more than most men I know."

Bandaging his hand with a few cloths and duct tape, there was little pause from Howard letting his entire hidden secret, and pent up feelings, out. "Then one day she told me I gotta change. She tried to convince me that she didn't cheat on me, and that you were mine and she said she couldn't live with who I had become. But she said she would leave you with me because you were my flesh and blood".

Shaking his head, as he looked at the floor and rubbed the back of his neck with his good hand, Howard muttered hostilities under his breath. As Liam attempted to hear, the words were inaudible to him.

"Only you ain't!" Mr. Heepen shrieked out again. "She left you with me so she could party and hook up with someone else, and take no responsibility for you! She left and dang near must've disappeared off the face of the earth, 'cuz she never has talked to me again, and I have searched high and low and can't find her."

"Pa, maybe she's right. Maybe I am yours. I know I'm yours, I love you! And I don't even care if I'm not yours... I love you. I want to stay with you. I'll clean up the mess. I'll take care of you and us. Please Pa, you couldn't!"

"I could and am. I made up my mind! I've held it all in for way too long. I can't take the hate anymore" he said sternly punching his bloody, poorly bandaged hand onto the table harder.

A surge in the electricity nearly coincided and then the lights and electronics all went silent as the power went out. Howard's silver, white, and grey hair peppered with a sprinkle of dark hairs still – and his matching moustache – were glistening in the streams of moon-light coming in through the windows in the tight kitchen-dining area.

"She was still young enough. I wasn't." his voice boomed another time. "I told her I'd done my duty with 5 boys. She said she understood but she never got to have her own. All she wanted was you. I could never forgive her. I had evidence. Still, I can't forgive her wherever she may be."

"Please Dad?"

"Stop callin' me that!" Howard screamed now walking to the sink to rinse off the blood on the rest of his arm and hands.

"Please then, can you give me any information that you have for mom and let me try to find her for a couple of days?"

"You better go quickly, before I change my mind like Pharaoh did when he set Moses free. I'll give you three days, and then I'm calling Utopia and reporting you as a runaway. Like I said, they take runaways."

"Thank you, Dad. I'm never going to stop loving you and I hope someday you can forgive me for not being yours and not getting to pick who I came to."

"Get outta here!!! Before I change my mind!" Howard hollered as he held his hand, which began bleeding through the cloth and past the haphazard duct tape. "I wish you luck!"

CHAPTER 7

"I can't take another step, Richard!" Lorraina hollered towards Richard who was 20 feet or so in front of her. "I'm going to die! It's too far and it smells awful and I'm thirsting to death and I'm going to die of thirstation."

Losing patience and full of irritation with her constant comments and stopping, Richard just kept on walking – his speed even increasing.

"Richard... did you hear me?" she said, dropping the suitcase and sleeping bag that she was carrying, and slumped down onto them.

"I heard you!" he yelled back, not even bothering to turn around; the space now was growing between them. "How could anyone unhear you?"

"Unhear is not a word." Lorraina said annoyed now too.

"Neither is thirstation! If you can make up words, I can too!" he said over his shoulder, slowing his pace a little. "And by the way," he started again, as he set down her other bags and turned back towards her a little, "You're not going to die from being thirsty!"

"How do you know?" she shouted back.

"Well for two reasons, well maybe three reasons. Number one reason is that if we don't get a 'move-on', the Utopia guards will find us and you'll die because they will kill you. It's almost 4:00 now, and if they haven't already... they will be watching the surveillance tapes. They are already likely heading out to find us, even if they don't watch the surveillance tapes, because I haven't come back from 'killing' you yet. They are going to wonder."

"What's number two then?" Lorraina snapped across the way.

"Number two: you haven't lost your voice yet. If you can still holler and complain you have enough spit left and aren't thirsting to death. Not yet anyway. So save your spit girl." Richard said, shaking his head in dismay at her lack of survival skills and what used to be known as "common sense" or general "know-how".

"And number three..." he went on with a bit of snarky ego, a little. "We are only less than a mile from the entrance of the water/sewage treatment facility, and you certainly won't die in less than a mile."

"But why does it matter if we get to a sewage plant?" Lorraina tilted her head and scrunched her nose up on one side of her face, in wonderment. "I'll still be thirsty, and I am absolutely NOT drinking sewage, no matter what!"

Again shaking his head in dismay at Lorraina's lack of knowledge in this field of his expertise, he just picked up her bags again and began walking.

"Wait up. Hey wait up!" Lorraina hollered and began getting up and gathering up her sleeping sack and luggage duffle-bag, with rollers. "Wait up!" she said, rushing after him. As she finally caught up, she said in an exhausted huff, "What do you know that I don't know?"

"A lot!" he said, glancing at her from the side, with an ever growing irritation.

"Like what?"

"Like that there is water there in the facility, even at the entrance, and it is clean water."

Lorraina's pace quickened at the thought of getting a drink of water fairly soon.

"How far have we come?" Lorraina began question barraging again. "Am I a fast walker? Do you think it will take us 10 minutes, 20, a half an hour?" No response was uttered. "What??? Hey what? Why are you rolling your eyes, and how come you aren't answering me?" She continued leaving barely a smidgen of time to answer her, even if he had wanted to.

"Hey Richard, did you hear me?" Still Richard offered no answers – not even a grunt or huff or anything – as he continued at an ever increasing rate. He was agitated, but that could only be seen by his eye rolls and facial expressions.

Lorraina was behind him and could not see that he was making any faces, so she assumed that he must not be replying, evidently because he could not hear her clearly enough.

"Richard, what's your last name again?" She inquired very loudly this time, in case he was beginning to go deaf. There was still no answer, she wondered if it was because she had asked toward his left ear, maybe she needed to ask next to his right ear, in case he was hard of hearing only in one ear.

Lorraina moved behind him attempting to keep up, to get to his right side, and not trip as she bumped, dragged, and tried to pull her rolling suitcase across medium sized rocks in the cracked, parched, powdery dust/sand combination of desert soil patches followed by cement like ground with random dips, divots, and twigs left over from sage brush or other haphazard wind-blown items.

Deafeningly, Lorraina started once more, "Richard, are you hard of hearing on one side?" she shrieked.

With everything in his soul, he tried to muster up more patience and did all he could to squish the desire to scream back at Lorraina for her to shut-up. He was a good man though, who was wise, had dealt with much, and with many people more irritating than Lorraina. Richard tried to respond with patience, even though to many, it may not have appeared like it.

"Lorraina, remember that I told you to save your spit? You are really going to need it!" he said, walking faster, his jaw tightening, his head held high, his neck out forward, as he moved faster ignoring her more. He was hoping this would stop her. He also was calculating plans in his head as to how to teach her some things about survival that would make a lasting impression.

"I know, I know, but I am pretty sure I will have enough, by the time we get to a refill. Spit, I mean!" Lorraina said completely undeterred from his reaction.

Realizing this, Richard barked out answers in a short tempered manner. "Ok then, the answers are:

1. Along the way
2. Yes
3. Depends on how fast we walk
4. Yes
5. Perecha
6. Nope
7. And any other answers to questions you ask... I am going to be ignoring you, so that I can save my spit!"

"That doesn't make sense." Lorraina piped up after a long pause and 20 minutes of their continued walking. "I can't remember all the questions I asked you, so your answers don't make any sense, except that your last name is Perecha" she paused for a second, very weak now, trying to catch her breath, and stay up with Richard.

"Well," she initiated again, "My last name was LaFleur. It is French, but we haven't lived in France for about 8 or 10 generations. Now my last name is Parsons, because my mom got remarried and my step-dad adopted me. I was 10 when that happened."

Richard grunted and continued plowing forward.

"It would sure be nice if you actually answered questions when I ask them, so that I know which answer belongs to which question."

"Well, I have answered enough questions for me. I am not one who enjoys getting interrogated." Richard responded a little nicer, but still exasperated. "So now I have one for you. How old are you anyway?"

"I'm 23." Lorraina blurted out, and then paused and thought about it, stopping her walking and everything, frozen in thought.

"How old are you?" She asked him the same question out of politeness, and wondering if she was supposed to, to be courteous.

"Sixty-eight years young, kiddo... and I'm most definitely old enough to be your grandpa. But I was just wondering because you actually remind me of my granddaughter, who is 15 and was just taken to Utopia.

"I'm a little confused," Richard began again. "Your personality seems similar to a 15 year old, not a 23 year old. I'm not saying that to cause offense... I have just never met someone your age who acted so... so, not your age" he paused in thought.

"I wonder," Richard began again, when Lorraina didn't respond. "If it is because you guys all went in there at age 15, and nobody taught you that you should be different or how to grow up?" he wondered out loud.

A sulky grimace struck Lorraina's face, nearly as if she had no control. "I find that very rude and as a personal attack, even if you say you didn't mean to be rude! I consider myself a very nice person and way more tolerant than most in Utopia, and yet I still think you are purposely trying to be offensive." Lorraina became rather defensive.

"What's to take offensively? Most people want to be younger or seem younger."

"I still think I..."

"Lay low!" Richard commanded, shoving Lorraina's head down and knocking her forward accidently. "Did you see that car? It just passed in the distance, and it's only going to take a couple of minutes to get here" he emphatically stressed.

"How do you know it's coming this way?" Lorraina asked, gathering her bags and helping herself up from her partial fall.

"I've worked here for years, it's the only road, and you have to turn off the main highway to get here."

"What do we do?" Lorraina questioned fearfully.

"We're finally here" Richard proclaimed, after racing to get open the hurricane style door that was slanting away from him at a slight angle and situated by itself. It lay positioned on the back side of a raised plateau of sand and reddish, beige dust that was so condensed that it had the appearance of cement or stucco. It was a mound jetting out of the ground away from the main facility and highly hidden due to the brush and terrain causing it to be camouflaged.

Dashing inside quickly, Richard and Lorraina heard the door slamming tightly behind them. It was utterly dark; neither of them could see one another, or even their own extremities. Richard knew his way around well, after six years of working half-time at this place, and often covering on holidays and weekends for many of his co-workers.

Their heavy panting and fearful breathing was audible, but still nothing was visible. Once the heartbeats and breathing slowed a little, some unfamiliar sounds were heard.

"What's that?" Lorraina's heart began speeding up again, fearfully demanding an answer.

"The pump. It's ok, it always makes that sound." Richard responded in a hurried whisper-yell. "Now be quiet, I'm listening".

"What is it pumping?" Lorraina answered, loudly as ever.

"The sewage of course, now be quiet!"

"Aren't we going to turn on some lights? I can't see," she still continued.

"Lorraina, no one can see and that is a blessing if you believe in God. That way the Utopia Security can't see us either."

"I thought you said there were no cameras here?" Lorraina questioned a little sarcastically.

"There are not, thank goodness, but the people in the car will be here soon."

"Then shouldn't we move?"

"I am moving" Richard responded with irritation, "and would you please stop talking and asking so many questions? It's making it hard for me to even think."

"Well, then please think faster, because this is freaking me out, and I talk even more and faster when I am nervous or scared"

"Wait here, I'll be back."

"Ok, but how will I know you're still there?"

"For crying out loud, young lady, where in the heck am I going to go?"

"Ok, ok, then just talk super quiet in a whisper, so I can know that you're still there".

"Or... I'll be quiet for the both of us. Let's play the quiet game." Richard said sarcastically, his harsh whisper fading off a little. Moving away from Lorraina in the solid darkness, he felt his way very quietly to the emergency supply box.

The emergency kit also held a flashlight, radio, first aid stuff, snacks, emergency food and more. He only removed the flashlight from the container and then quickly turned it on.

"Finally I can see" Lorraina shouted excitedly.

"Do you not understand the meaning of being quiet, woman?" Richard whispered almost angrily.

"Sorry," Lorraina whispered loudly this time. "So where is the water?" she whisper-whined.

"I'm working on it, one thing at a time." Richard walked around a corner with Lorraina quickly tagging along behind him.

"Water!" she hollered, again forgetting the importance of remaining silent in this crucial situation. "I see a water bottle." She dashed forward darting towards the small cheap plastic water bottle, snatching it off of the top of a metal box near a rusty old hand pump.

Almost as quickly as she had grabbed the sole container of water, Richard carefully but forcefully took it from her. "This..." he said breathing heavily "is not for you."

"What! You're going to drink it all for yourself?"

"Of course not... it's not for either of us. It is the primer water. The pump that you hear is the sewage lift and the equipment that handles the sewer system. This pump is the hand pump that must be primed" Richard paused and tried to work up some spit in his mouth in order to gulp.

"If you drink this water, that's the rest of our water, and that won't last more than a few seconds. If we use that water for the hand-pump to prime it, then we will have as much water as we like."

Perplexed was the look on Lorraina's face, it was obvious that she'd never heard of priming or anything very mechanical and Richard had no time or patience to really explain it to her at that moment.

"I can see that you are very confused, but you can look it up on Google later. You had better not use your cell phone now or they'll track us. I already shut mine off."

"Well mine is already long dead and if it wasn't, I would have used it as a flashlight." Lorraina said, sadly, in a sarcastic whisper.

Richard opened the cap of the water bottle and was about to pour it into the pump, when he froze momentarily.

"What's wrong?... What are you waiting for?" Lorraina said frantically, hovering near.

"I can barely refrain from attacking you and grabbing that water." She said nearly ferociously.

Richard looked seriously concerned in thought and placed the cap back onto the water bottle. "You couldn't succeed anyway, so don't bother" Richard said, scarcely caring about the threat and not even looking at her.

Lorraina frantically began speaking louder than a whisper in a rapid, almost unintelligible manner. "In the movie *Karen Karina Kevlar: Dinosaur Defender*, Karen is willing to go hungry to save a baby dinosaur, but Braden Bjorn just eats her food, kills the baby dinosaur and all of its' babies that are about to hatch."

Looking at nothing, she continued after a quick breath. "I'm wanting and trying to be like Karen, but I really just totally understand Braden right now. I don't think that I even can be Karen. So, just PLEASE, PLEASE GIVE ME THE WATER!" she tantrum-scream-demanded, reaching for the water bottle.

"We have no time for this garbage and nonsense." Richard said dodging away from Lorraina and shutting the flashlight off. "Seems like you are actually being a Karen to me" Richard responded sarcastically, under his breath a little, in the dark.

"I'm sorry!" She said. "Turn it back on. I'm scared and thirsty and it's actually cold in here. Why won't you let me have water, or do whatever you have to do to get the water working? I'm sorry, I just need a rest and water!" she said as she began sobbing.

Richard turned the flashlight back on. "Lorraina" he said calmly, controlled, and in a very serious tone. "You need to think! Breathe calmly... I can hear them. They are coming in in a few seconds. They are putting in the code." he listed off short commands.

"Do not scream Lorraina, but there is a huge tarantula behind you and you need to run. Follow me as fast and quiet as you can."

He had already picked up her bags in the dark, when he first heard them. He ran quietly and quickly. She ran even faster passing him up down the long dirt floored corridor into the darkness.

CHAPTER 8

Hiding quietly behind massive cylinder shaped sewage tanks, Richard and Lorraina were again completely in the dark. That is, other than the green, blue, and red lights on the various sensors, batteries, and equipment.

It was silent aside from the beeps and sounds of motors, churning sewage, the sound of large fans, and circulation pumps. Both of them had their shirts up over their noses – not only to drown out the permeating stench – but attempting to hide the reflection of light that was bouncing off of their faces.

"I'm so scared!!!" Lorraina whispered in a horrified scarcely audible whisper. "What if that tarantula followed us in here, or what if there are more of them?" she whispered now terrifying herself.

"I'm sure we're safe!" he whispered commandingly. "Try not to think about it."

"How can I do that??? Try not to think about it?!?! That's like someone saying try not to think of your eye getting poked out while they have you strapped to a table for eye surgery and the drill is coming at your eye!" she whisper-yelled.

"Shhhh" Richard said and looked out from behind the tank a little. "I have good ears, I hear them again."

They held very still and put all but the very top of their heads into their shirts and waited. They could hear mumbling and talking and almost passive joking conversation going on. They remained still and tried to listen harder.

"This is so ridiculous... what a waste of time." One of the men touted loud enough to be heard.

"I'm sure they just hitchhiked, Grady." The other security man responded.

"Or Richard called his wife and got a ride."

"Yah right, give me a break you idiot! If he's gonna get his first chance to be like us, and get to do the killings, he's gonna have fun with it. He's not gonna call his wife and ask for a ride" Jace shook his head at Grady and half smacked the back of his head.

"He's always had a look of jealousy towards us. She's young, he's old... and he's a tough guy" Jace continued. "He's gonna have fun! Let him, man. She was annoying and then one less brat left from the Utopia project."

"So, Jace are you gonna have fun with this girl?" Grady questioned.

"Heck no! Well, I'll have fun with her, but not like you think, man. She's ugly, man. She's not my type. I do not dig afros and sass!" Jace said in a bigoted fashion, showing his obvious distaste for individuals of African descent.

Jace Cobrin was the head security officer, and he was a sickening and hateful animal, who loved his job. He very much disliked his superior, Mr. Avera, but only because he was jealous.

"Well, one way or another I'm done with this assignment, Grady boy." Jace said, patronizingly and talking down to his coworker, who was maybe three to five younger than he, at most.

"I told him to go kill her. I don't care how long he takes, maybe he'll be more cheerful tomorrow when he comes back to work" Jace went on. "If Mr. Avera has an issue about this, he can take it up with me."

"Part of our right as men in the security guard, promised by Mr. Avera, was we were also allowed to play out our fantasies in reality. We get to have fun too!"

"He knows he could never keep up this illusion or get away with this scheme if he didn't have our help. You know that the laws are not the same out of Utopia, unless you get the right cop, who has already bought-in."

"I know, I know. I get it. I just don't want Mr. Avera turning on us and turning us in for our crimes." said Grady.

"Grady... if Mr. Avera dares, he'll be destroyed. I have way too much dirt on him; including video footage of him killing babies and young kids, not just 15-year olds and up, and tons of them too."

"What are you thinking of doing, Jace?"

"That's Captain Cobrin to you, Grady."

"Sorry, Captain. I just don't understand what you're planning, or what you are trying to say to me."

"I'm not planning anything at all, except covering my back. This gives me more freedom to do whatever I please. Mr. Avera can't do anything about it, because I'll tell the authorities outside of Utopia. This puts me on equal or higher footing. Anyhow, the only reason that I want Richard Perecha to kill someone too, is so that he can have no dirt on me. So, I'm giving him as much time as he wants."

"What if he is not back for 2 days? Mr. Avera will be very angry."

"I don't care if he takes a week, if he wants to take that long with her, in my opinion. I will cover for him myself, if I have to. Now... let's go handle that stupid sassy friend of hers. I have a great idea!"

"Yes sir, Captain Cobrin. Yes sir!" Their voices began to fade, and disappear in the distance, as they chatted about how Richard couldn't possibly be there because he would have used the water, or taken the car if he had walked there, and neither was changed.

Richard popped his eyes and face out of his shirt opening and took in a deep breath. He looked at Lorraina somberly, feeling fatherly compassion for her. He was angry at his co-workers sickening comments and felt guilt that she had had to hear all of the men's filth; even though he knew that he had no intention of doing – or even thinking – any of those things that they had mentioned.

"Lorraina," he whispered, hearing her snuff her nose now, and cry very quietly. "Are you ok?"

"No..." she whisper-sobbed. "Of course, I'm not ok! You are actually planning to kill me!?" she asked and stated simultaneously.

"They are about to torture and kill my best friend for no apparent reason. And I'm so thirsty that I'm literally licking my tears to wet my mouth enough to keep my throat from killing me anymore. And... and there are tarantulas in here and I think I'm going to die of a stroke!" her voice was beginning to get louder as she assumed the men were gone.

"Lorraina... I am not like those men. Not at all! The look on my face – that they presume as jealousy – is actually disgust. I am sickened by them all, but I needed a job to protect and take care of my family. Plus I am trying to keep an eye on my grandkids, who have been taken to Utopia. I want to see what goes on here, so I can see where all of the children are disappearing to and my grandchildren specifically" Richard defended himself calmly in a reassuring voice.

"I could never kill you, or anyone for that matter. Not unless I had to, and that would only be in self-defense. I had to swear a pledge to Mr. Avera that I would help him with his plan – that you don't even want to know about, that my wife doesn't even know about – in order to work for Utopia. But just because he gave me permission to "take what I want and abuse and kill who I want" doesn't mean that I will. I won't, because

I don't want to, Lorraina!" Richard elevated his voice in an emphatic whisper.

Richard paused briefly and looked at the floor. He then slipped out from behind the sewage tanks and held out his hand for Lorraina, in order to help her up, out from behind the tanks.

"This is a problem, however, because the men are starting to think that I am a spy – which I basically am – but if they figure that out, then I'm dead. I mean actually dead, they are not kidding around. They do kill people. And if I am dead, you are definitely dead, and then no one can help stop Mr. Avera and this awful city of corruption."

"What are we going to do about Krista then? Is there anything we can do to save her?"

"I'm not sure, I think we're safe to head up to the surveillance room now and see what they are doing out there."

"I thought you said that they didn't record in here?"

"They don't. Not inside, but outside they have surveillance. They don't record, but they have a room where you can look out and see on camera what's going on. If you are in here, you could push record... but it doesn't record on its own."

"I'm scared, weak, and I really actually NEED water NOW to be able to do anything to help Krista or anyone."

"We'll stop and get some water on the way up."

Lorraina nodded and held out her hand for assistance. "I sure hope that tarantula is gone by now."

"Ha-ha... about that, Lorraina... I have to tell you the truth about that. There was no tarantula. I needed you to run fast and stop talking and I did hear you say you were scared of spiders" Richard admitted.

"How could you? How can I trust you now?"

"I'm sorry Lorraina, I really am, but you didn't realize how scared that you should be of the Utopia security guards – and I had no time to explain! I needed to have you run, if I was going to save you. You should trust me, because not only is there no other way, but if I was going to hurt you, and was like those men, then obviously I would have hurt you by now."

"But why couldn't you let me have water first? Why did you look scared and put the cap back on? I thought it was the tarantula this entire time."

Richard and Lorraina had been walking back towards the water pump as they talked, and were nearly there by then. Richard began to explain himself to this drained young woman, who now had begun to really remind him of his granddaughter. "I simply had realized that if they saw water near the pump on the floor, they would recognize that we had been here, or were here, and that we wouldn't have enough time to pump the water anyhow. Sorry!"

"I might be able to forgive you – because that means no tarantulas."

CHAPTER 9

"What you are describing to me sounds like something we call PTSD or Post-Traumatic Stress Disorder, Bridget." Jarom Freeman said in a deep masculine voice. "Have you ever heard of PTSD Bridget?" he genuinely wanted to know, toward the end of the session.

"No, I really haven't. Am I supposed to know about it?" Bridget asked, embarrassed.

"Many individuals who have left Utopia have been seeking therapists, Ms. Buchanan. Sometimes, just to learn things that they missed while in Utopia; things that others would have learned by these ages. They want to be able to learn and fill in the holes and gaps of the outside world in a safe environment where they are not being mocked." Jarom Freeman explained in a kind and professional manner.

"But how did you miss out on Utopia? It seems that you are close in age to me?" Bridget asked sincerely.

"Well, I'm not really supposed to share my personal life with my clients, but I will say that I was already well into my 18th year when Utopia was founded and officially launched. At that time – I know that it's not that way now – individuals had a choice whether they wanted to go to Utopia or not. I opted not, as I was already graduated and had college plans. Now the mandatory cut off age is 21 – and they are even talking about upping it to 25."

"No... That's horrible! Then I'd be stuck in there still. I hope they can't get away with that. This is taking away more agency from people. They've already taken almost everything from me. Can't somebody stop them?"

"Unfortunately, I can't answer that question because not only is it opinion based, but we're out of time for our counseling session today. Do you want to follow up with me or a psychologist?"

"I thought you were a psychologist?"

"No, I'm working on my PHD, but for now, I'm a counselor or therapist. Our facility can set you up with prescriptions if you need, or just work with you as we did today; whichever you feel that you need."

"I don't know what I need... That's what I'm here for. But, if even a little kid could figure out that I am messed up, or weird, or obsessed with shoes, than I think that a counselor should be able to figure it out! I just don't know. I just need to tell somebody and have them help me make sense of it all."

"Well, it sounds like I can do that. We can schedule for next week if you like."

"Yes, sounds good."

Bridget checked her calendar on her device, set a time with this charming, suave counselor and walked out feeling like an idiot. "I can't believe I just told him so much", she whispered under her breath to herself. Her thoughts were interrupted by a loud announcing of the next client.

"Hayden Baulmfield, next please." Bridget looked up as she saw his dusty, worn-out tennis shoes heading towards her to head back for his counseling appointment. As she glanced up, she made eye contact momentarily and Hayden froze instantly.

This stranger, to her, stood staring now, his eyes popped wide open. She stepped back a couple of steps and appeared frightened. "What?" She questioned in a bit of an alarmed tone.

"You've got the kinesis in your eyes!" Hayden said in a creepy, evil tone – hunching his body and scrunching his shoulders like a deranged beast.

"You are playing tricks on me! I never knew you were real, or that you were going to follow me to my counseling appointments. You already warned me and you already ruined my best performance yet!" his voice grew ever intense and furious. "And where is your Gaelic regalia now? You FREAK!!!" Hayden roared into Bridget's face.

"That's enough!" Mr. Freeman said boldly in an authoritative manner. "I take it the two of you know each other?" Jarom asked, looking inquisitively at Bridget. "And don't get along that well?" he concluded.

"No sir!" Bridget began. "I have never seen this man before in my entire life. This is my first encounter and I am quite scared" she said, rather shaky and darting back behind Jarom's shoulder partway.

"I don't want him following me or knowing anything about me, please!" Bridget pled in enough fear to nearly draw up tears.

"You're such a liar Tyrnia, *The Woman of Woes*! You even stocked me in my dreams!" Hayden said, pointing at Bridget as he climbed onto a chair to try and force her to look at him.

"Ok, that's enough Mr. Baulmfield! You head into my office now or we're going to have to call the authorities." Mr. Freeman commanded, pointing into his office.

Hayden glared at Bridget as he walked backwards into the office, still staring and glaring Bridget down the entire way.

Mr. Freeman pulled the door shut calmly from the outside and left Hayden in the room by himself momentarily. He turned on the privacy fan to help aid in confidentiality. Leaning toward Bridget a little, lowering his voice in front of the waiting room occupants, he began to ask a few more questions.

"Do you promise that you have never, ever, met this man before?" he asked in all seriousness. "I really need to know that, and need complete honesty. I need to know if you have ever met him, know him, he was an old boyfriend, etc. I can help you..."

"No doctor... nothing like that" Bridget answered defensively. "I promise... I have never met him before! I promise! In fact, I can't even recollect even seeing him before."

"Ok, I believe you," Jarom said. A slight half-smirk crossed his face, suddenly, and he looked at the floor a little, trying not to make eye contact and thinking to himself.

"What's so funny about this situation, Doctor?" she snapped, feeling a little irritated.

"Oh it has nothing to do with that guy. I am sorry. It's just that you can't call me doctor yet. I like hearing it, so it brings a smile to my face. I was always planning to be a doctor, so I like it. But... I am not a doctor yet" Jarom finished, straightening up and being more professional; realizing that he'd gained an entire audience now. He glanced around quickly and got back into his boring therapist mode.

"I will note that, in your file, and I will see to it that your schedules do not overlap ever again" he continued. "I will keep him here long enough that he won't know what vehicle you are leaving in, so he won't be able to follow you." Jarom paused, for a quick breath.

Glancing around himself, he noticed that all the patients were leaning forward and attempting to get a better shot at hearing the conversation and he wasn't sure just how much they all could hear, even though they were whispering.

"Patient privacy is of utmost importance to us" he said loud enough for the waiting room individuals to hear, and placing his hand on her shoulder slightly, prodding her towards a hall near the reception window. This area was a bit more secure and less likely for people to overhear, although they could all still see.

"Should I call you Mr. Freeman then? Or what should I call you, if you are not a doctor?" Bridget said, still attempting to stop blushing as she scanned the room and saw two elderly women tilting very far forward to watch and attempt to hear them.

"Mr. Freeman is just fine, or you are welcome to call me Jarom, if you wish. I'm fine with a first name basis. I do have to ask you to please not repeat my client's name to any of your family and friends, unless you absolutely have to. I encourage you to call the authorities if you are concerned or feel that you are being stalked or anything of that nature".

"Do you think he would stalk me?" Bridget asked scrunching her face up a bit in fear.

"I don't know. He has never acted this way before, and normally he seems pretty calm. I can't divulge much more than that, but you never know sometimes with people. I've definitely been learning that in this occupation," he rested again for a split second.

"Bridget, I don't ever give out my number to anyone from work... but I feel personally responsible for your safety. I want to ensure that you are ok".

"No, that's ok, you really don't have to. I don't want you to feel awkward or break any rules or anything. I will just call the office if there is an emergency or I need help" she said, feeling uncomfortable, as she watched the front desk worker's eyes dart up and pop wide open.

"No one will be at the office if you need to call after hours. I'm getting a work cell phone anyway, very soon, for emotional and mental health emergencies of course" he said now, stuttering a little nervous and awkward himself. "Until then, this is my number" he continued abruptly, writing his number on the back of a business card that he had grabbed from the front desk.

Looking up at her, he saw the secretaries at the front desk staring, still with their jaws nearly dropping. "Please don't call unless it is urgent or you are in danger, or if you are scared that you're in danger. I hope that everything will be ok and I look forward to seeing you at our next appointment. Now I need to get in there with him and make sure that he's ok," he concluded, turning sharply and noticing all the snoopy onlookers, who quickly sat straight up in their seats.

CHAPTER 10

"Mr. Baulmfield, what is going on with you today?" Jarom asked, in a polite yet powerful manner, holding out a dinner-mint candy-dish to Hayden.

"No way, Jarom! That is disgusting!!! Other people touched their bare hands in that dish, and got their germs all over the rest of those candies!" Hayden fixated on the germs and not on the situation he had just created.

"You should know that, and know how dangerous germs are, in your profession!" Hayden snapped a little at Mr. Freeman. "And you took forever; our appointment is halfway over already!"

"You may have asked me to call you by your first name, but I prefer not to be called by my first name with my clients. So, it is Mr. Freeman if you please?"

Mulling things over, Mr. Freeman decided to mention a few things Hayden had just brought up instead of skipping over them. "Hayden, you mentioned that I should know that people have left germs in the dinner-mint container. You implied that you do not like that. It seemed as though you felt that I should be able to read your mind and know that."

Jarom was now in a teacher mode, "Yes, I do know that there are germs in this container and that there are germs nearly everywhere, but most people are able to work through the thought of that because they want something sweet and realize that they can get just as many germs from taking a breath."

Jarom continued, "I am not a mind reader Hayden, and no-one is... So, I want you to realize that no one can read minds, they can only guess. So, you need to be honest with me and others!"

Hayden was now playing with the blinds and lifting them up and down and twisting them open and shut. Jarom tried to ignore Hayden's behavior and just keep talking.

"Also, I am sorry that I took a while, but you really scared that girl out there. Why did you do that Hayden? I have never seen you act like this before. How do you even know the woman that you were talking to, out in the waiting area?"

"She snuck into my dream" Hayden began, as Jarom's eyebrow rose on one side. "It seemed so real, I really thought it was real, until my dog woke me up. It was one of the best dreams that I have ever had, except for her... she ruined it!"

"How did she ruin it?" Jarom asked, attempting to hide his look of concern.

"I was about to let a ton of baby dinosaurs eat everyone and she warned me not to."

"That sounds pretty intense!"

"Oh, you don't believe me? Are you mocking me?" Hayden paused extremely briefly. "I already said it was a dream! I am aware that it isn't true yet!"

"Yet?" the counselor gave an extremely inquisitive look, raising one eyebrow again and cocking his head slightly. "What do you mean when you say 'yet'? Are you suggesting that you are planning, and capable of having baby dinosaurs eat everyone?"

"Not just that, but now I'm convinced that Tyrnia, *Woman of Woes* is after me, and going to try to thwart my plans and successes. I'm sick of all the naysayers, and was about to have them all killed!"

"Hayden, what are the naysayers' names? Did you meet any of them in your dreams too, or in real life?"

"You think I'm just making all this up, don't you? You just think you're so much smarter than me, like you're so suave and great and smarter and like you've always been perfect and never once thought of a bad thing in your life. And you're just so charitable and so wonderful, and like I'm the only killer out there in my dreams and like you're so high and mighty and you've never killed anyone in your dreams before, right?!?!? Right?!?!?"

Hayden began escalating intensely, in a way very unlike him. Jarom had never seen him behave in this manner before. The conduct was very off for his regular personality, and was terribly alarming. Mr. Freeman knew that he needed to help Hayden de-escalate, and he needed to get some help for himself too.

"Did you change anything recently?" Jarom questioned calmly acting as if nothing was wrong and as if here were not alarmed or concerned, giving no reaction as much as possible. "Did you fall or have someone pass away unexpectedly these last two weeks?"

"Since I've last seen you?" Jarom continued slowly, as he leaned toward his desk and wheeled closer, getting a notebook and Hayden's chart.

He pretended his pen didn't work and rummaged in his desk with one hand while simultaneously pushing an emergency alarm button that called the police and alerted the front desk with his other hand. He found another pen and jotted down the date and Hayden's full name, waiting for a response from Hayden.

"I don't know! Why are you asking me that?"

"Are you the counselor or am I?" Jarom said calmly. "I do have reasons for my questions and I can guarantee that my plan is only in your best interest and to help you." Jarom paused momentarily, looking at his notebook and thinking.

"When did you first start thinking about getting rid of the naysayers?" He asked seriously.

"Not until my dream a couple days ago." Hayden responded quickly.

"When have you thought about it afterward?"

"Almost constantly!"

"Have you ever been diagnosed with anything other than high functioning Autism/Asperger's before? Any mania, bi-polar, paranoia, schizophrenia etc.?"

"No, no, nothing like that! What are you trying to say, Doc?" Hayden scoffed mockingly. "That I'm crazy! That you're scared?!?! Ha ha ha ha ha bwahahahaha!!" Hayden now cackled so loud that the people in the waiting room could hear and his noise level was clearly audible even over the privacy fan.

The elderly secretary came out from behind the desk and quietly told the clients that there was a safety concern and that they needed to please slowly exit the waiting room. One middle aged man with a grumpy, dominant attitude responded, "That punk isn't going to ruin or alter my schedule today. Nobody messes with me or my routine, or they will have my fist to explain to."

The other clients began rapidly filing out of the exit with alarmed expressions, just as the office door flew open and Hayden came bursting out. As he walked out, he saw everyone leaving, aside from the one tough-man. Hayden said, "What is going on here? A fire drill? We used to have these as kids in school... I loved these."

"This is no fire drill, hot shot!" the grumpy, feisty man snapped. "You enjoy making a scene and scaring people and getting attention and forcing everyone to drop everything for you, just like that. You ruin their plans... change their schedules etc., just because you're on a whim today, Mr. Know-it-all. Well, it's not working for this guy here! Nope, no sir, it's not working for Travis

Worthington. Not happening! I'm waiting right here," he said, folding his arms in an irritated huff.

"Hi, my name is Jake!" Hayden said holding his hand out to Mr. Worthington in a weird hysterical manner, expecting the man to shake his hand. "Don't tell anyone that my real name is Hayden, ok?" He then cackled as if all social etiquettes had been forgotten.

Then, even Travis Worthington, the waiting-room grump, was scared and realized that Hayden was completely delusional and eerily unstable. He reached up and began to shake Hayden's hand, as Hayden leaned over his chair – scarcely four inches from his face – which was unexpected, and rather intimidating to him.

As Travis shook Hayden's hand, Hayden yanked it towards himself a little. "You can call me Jake, so I don't get in trouble, on the double. Oh, and you can fax me, but never tax me!" Hayden creepily babbled.

"Wow, that actually rhymed," Hayden continued, as the authorities finally came rushing forward through the doors, and grasped both his arms, as calmly and gently as possible. Hayden was not even trying to resist them, just cackling and laughing hysterically, saying strange things that made no sense.

CHAPTER 11

In all her glory, as she was preparing to set, the glistening sun refracted magnificent hues of pink, yellow, and orange onto the cotton-candy like clouds. The rushing, crashing, and roaring of the ocean was glorious to Bridget's ears after a long and crazy day.

Her day had been rough, not only due to her strange incident with Hayden, but due to a shipment of merchandise having come in at her small shop. "Your Bridge by the Ocean / A Bridge to Wellness and Hope", her sign read above the door as she pulled it shut. She was exhausted after stocking shelves, organizing, rearranging pricing, and making more room for her new oils, remedies, elixirs and such. All her other merchandise, including new t-shirts with her store name on them, took a while to unload.

Bridget walked slowly down the boardwalk in front of her store after locking up. No other motion or sound was heard other than the sea. It was just her and the exquisite aroma of the salty waves in the distance, everyone else had gone home for the day. She had stayed a little late and was just about to head "home" to her parent's house, but needed the peace and rejuvenation that the ocean and nature give so beautifully and freely.

Her car was a ways off in the distance and she was in no rush to get to it. Her pace slowed to a stop and she closed her eyes, lifted her head a little, and smelled the ocean breeze. She breathed in through her nose long and deep, her hands and arms gently rising, absorbing the moment.

Opening her eyes, Bridget just gazed at the gorgeous sunset and began walking again slowly as the wind started to pick up. She got her phone out to call her mom; she did this often now that they had been able to reunite, after her time in Utopia. Her mother, Gena, had become extremely protective and a tad-bit paranoid after losing her daughter like that, with no word, for so many years.

"Hey Mom, I guess you're busy" Bridget said to the voicemail. "I guess I'll try again later, or see you when I get there. I'm running a little late; just start the party without me. Tell Brady I'm sorry. I know this birthday is a big deal, I swear I'll be there, just late... I have something fun for him too. Ok, I gotta get driving, see you guys soon."

After hanging up, Bridget switched her phone over to camera mode and held it up to take a few shots of the sky, before the colors all dissipated and the sky would become lightless. At that moment a creaking of the boardwalk was heard. As Bridget darted herself around and tripped back a step, to see what was behind her – her phone slipped from her hand, and right through the open slat in the boardwalk.

Her mind creating dreadful images of the creaking noise being Hayden Baulmfield – coming to kill her – Bridget scarcely wanted to open her eyes and see what or who it was. As she resisted the urge to keep her eyes shut tight, she was looking straight ahead and saw the top of a young boys head. She glanced down, recognizing her young friend from the store a few days before. "Oh my gosh! You scared me nearly to death young man! My heart was almost leaping out of me, it almost tore through!" Bridget squeaked in alarm and panic.

"I'm sorry!" Liam said sincerely, "I didn't mean to make you drop your phone or scare you."

"Well, what are you here for? I'm pretty sure you know that I'm closed already for the day, don't you?"

"I do! I know that" Liam responded confidently, but with forlorn eyes.

"Is everything alright?" Bridget asked calming down and sensing that his fear, remorse and solemn demeanor was more intense than hers.

"I'm looking for my mom?" Liam's voice cracked as he attempted to keep himself from tearing up again. It was apparent – now that Bridget was paying attention – that Liam had been crying for quite some time.

"Well, where did you last see her?" Bridget wanted to quickly resolve the problem and get on her way to see her own family.

"Right here, on your sidewalk!" He said sadly.

"What? When? I've been here all day and I haven't seen hardly a soul. What was she wearing?" Bridget continued, perplexed and hurried.

"It was four years or so ago, Ma'am. She was wearing a black felt type dress coat with silver buttons up the front. She had a light bluish, greenish, gray scarf that was flying in the wind. She had an ocean colored skirt that touched her toes. I remember looking at her toes a lot, and they were painted the same color. That must have been her favorite color." Liam stopped, staring at the ground where her feet had been.

Bridget had no idea what to say, but was confused about the situation and needed to know more to help him. "Liam, where did your mother go after that? Where did she work? Did she and your dad get divorced? Did she die? Is it just you and your dad?" Bridget flooded his mind with questions.

"I don't know if she died. We never heard that. Daddy says she ran away and left us, but I don't know where she went. She worked here at your shop, except it had a different name and different stuff in it too" Liam responded in a tone of frustration.

"She stood here waving goodbye, hugging me, saying 'Be good for your daddy son. He is your daddy, don't let him fool you. You are so like him in the good ways. Keep the good and throw out all the bad ways'." Liam paused, fighting back new tears. He gulped hard and then began again.

"Then she gently pushed me towards him and said, 'I have to close up shop now, go with your father. I will always love you and him too!' Then my dad hollered at me to go with him, and left without a word to mama, only a long silent glare over his shoulder. As far as I know they have never spoken since, although he says that he has tried to look for her. I never saw her again."

"So, it's just you and your dad, or do you have siblings?" Bridget questioned, now sincerely concerned versus trying to just fix a problem.

"Actually," Liam began, lowering his head toward the floor and acting nervous and agitated, "It's just me... not me and my dad." He waited briefly, and then glanced up quickly, while his face was still towards the ground, he finished, "My dad kicked me out last night."

"Why? I thought you seemed close and he told you a lot of things he believed?"

"I was close to him, I did everything for him, I loved him, I looked up to him... but he didn't do any of those things for me. He doesn't even love me or want me or even like me!" He was staring at the ground without blinking, his eyes welling up with tears of anger, pain, betrayal, and even a tinge of hate.

"He said I'm not his son. He said my mom cheated on him and he can't stand me anymore, because I remind him of her and that she cheated." Liam raced through his words, stumbling over them and breathing in and out while he was talking in a frantic, heart-racing pace.

"I know my momma wouldn't lie! I just know it! I trust her! She told me to believe her no matter what he said. I tried to trust him, but he was not caring, or loving. He kicked me out, he says he'll only give me three days to find her and then he's calling Utopia and telling them that I'm a runaway!"

"What? How could anyone do that?" Bridget questioned, as she compassionately touched his upper arm.

"He says that he checked with them and that they will take kids as young as me if they are bad, or they're runaways or even if their parents don't want them anymore!" Liam turned away, angrily yanking his arm away from Bridget, and pulling back, as if it were she that he was angry with.

"I'm sorry Liam... I was trying to show you that I care. I wasn't trying to hurt you or scare you." Bridget conveyed with her words and body language, as she crouched down to be closer to his level, hoping to lessen any fear he might have.

"I don't know what to say Liam, except he can't! He can't because I won't let him. I don't know anything about your father, but I will not let Utopia take you. I've been there before. I lived there. It was appalling and I pledge to you, right now, that I will personally do anything and everything within my power to ensure that you stay out of Utopia." Bridget expounded as she stayed sitting on her heels.

"Why, why would you do something like that for me?"

"For the same reason that I have a free-bin in my store, Liam" Bridget began, as the wind intensified and the rain started to pour down upon them. "I want to help people to NEVER have to feel the pain that I have felt, to never have to experience the things that I have experienced. I have lived through the nightmare of Utopia, and I want to ensure that no one, especially innocent children, would ever, ever, ever have to go to that evil, horrid, hell-like prison. It was the worst four years of my life!" She began crying, her tears now blending with the rain that was streaming down her face from her drenched, disheveled hair.

"Do you promise you're not my mom?" Liam said now throwing himself at her and wrapping his soaking arms around her neck, hugging her so tightly that he could almost choke her. She reciprocated, wrapping her arms around him, but pulling back enough to breathe. She held him briefly, wanting to hold and comfort him, but getting very cold and doused with rain-water.

"Your mom?" Bridget began, slowly pulling back halfway, still grasping his biceps in her hands. She was looking him in the eyes clearly now, just gazing inquisitively, with the concern visible in her stare.

"I don't understand." She finally stated calmly, not breaking the gaze. "Why would you think that I'm your mother, Liam? Do you not remember her, or what she looked like anymore?"

"I do, I do remember! I will never forget! I think you are my mother, because you look exactly like her. I think you must have gotten amnesia or something. I read about it once and it's where you hit your head and forget everything. Why can't you remember me mom? Did you get hit or fall?" Bridget pulled away rapidly and stood up, her face became worried, hesitant, then cross.

"Did someone put you up to this young man? Is your father's name, Hayden, by chance?" She raised her voice, pointing a finger at him in the ever increasing rain.

"This isn't funny Liam! I'm scared! I have no phone now, it's probably ruined due to all this rain, and I'm supposed to be miles away from here right now at my mom's house for my brother's birthday, before they take him away and send him off to Utopia. I'm already sick over that. Then some crazy lunatic man tells me that he knows me from his dreams, and now you are saying I have amnesia and am your mother!"

Bridget looked down at the ground and tried to regroup and control her fear and wide range of other emotions. "I have never had any children!" She cleared her throat. "I told you that the other day. I'm only 25 years old, how could I have given birth to you? I would have had to have had you when I was only 14."

"I have heard of that before, but my dad did say my mom was 36 when she had me" Liam stopped for a moment just staring at her, both of them soaking through and beginning to shiver from the strong wind.

"I don't understand!" Liam said, fighting his anger and tears, his eyes scrunched, attempting to wipe the rain-water away with his soaking sleeve. "You look exactly like her" he cried. "And you work in her shop and I've watched you almost every day for years, ever since you reopened the store."

Liam's voice had escalated into a yelling mixed with crying to be heard above the waves crashing. He wanted to be audible above what had become a storm. "I've waited every day for you here, every day since you left me. Why did you leave us? It has to be you!" Liam cried out, the loudest he had yet in an explosive emotion filled state.

"Oh Liam, I wish I could say it was me, to comfort you! I wish I could fix your pain. I lost my mom for years and know part of your pain, but I did find her eventually. I will help you find your mom, but we've got to get inside before we get sick from this weather" she shouted through the ever increasing wind.

"I have a small apartment off the back of the shop, Liam, and there is that bin of free clothes. We've got to get dry then we'll talk about this, ok?" Bridget held out her hand to Liam and began fumbling around, trying to get her keys to go back inside.

CHAPTER 12

Pouring in the last drop of water from the bottle, to prime the pump, Richard began pumping the lever up and down. He began pumping harder and faster and then handed the empty water bottle to Lorraina. "Hold it here and when the water comes out you can fill it."

Lorraina took the bottle weakly now, shaking a bit, and waited nervously, trying to trust that there would be water. She wanted to believe there would be, but had never seen anything like that before. Hoping that the guards would not come back... and especially that there were no tarantulas, Lorraina waited.

The glimmer of the lights in the hall, that Richard had finally turned on, were glistening gloriously off of the water as it began gushing out. The water came out so fast that it knocked the bottle right out of Lorraina's hand. Diving forward, without a thought of anything else, Lorraina stuck her face into the downpour, right up near the spout. She began chugging water very awkwardly and manner free.

Richard kept pumping the water, allowing her to drink for a time, and then in military-fashion barked orders. "Now, grab that water bottle and refill it so that I can have some too. Then find the bucket, that we left near the utility sink, so that we can fill it." She hurried and did as he asked, handed him the water bottle, he guzzled it rapidly and then handed it back to her.

"You need to refill that straight away" Richard commanded. "Then fill the bucket. After that, I am going to be ready to take a break, so can you trade?"

"I'll try" Lorraina said, "I've never really done anything like this before...I'm not sure I am strong enough. I am a weakling, I'm told. I can't even get my water bottle lid off; it's too hard for me."

She paused from speaking, to fill the water bottle and bucket, and then continued, "But I do recall that in one of my favorite movies that one girl does try, one time, to be different from everyone around her, and she does lift something heavy. Of course, she does get mocked and stopped because she is being weird and different. But that movie gave me hope that I could be different than everyone else. It's called..."

"I really don't care what it's called right now! What do you guys do in Utopia, just sit around watching movies? Didn't you ever work or exercise or play sports or anything?"

"'Sports cause jealousy and contention' we were taught... And exercise makes people sick – some scientists have discovered that, and 'movies are very educational' they say." Lorraina took a quick breath and continued. "We learned in school that you would have to write over 1,000 words just to explain what our teachers said could be displayed in one still frame of a movie. So, it's just a waste of time to read or write or do school the old way. We have learned so much more and become so much more efficient by using only movies and video footage, I'm sure."

"You just drank sewage!" Richard said with a smirk and stopped pumping. He turned his back and began to walk off, up to the control room.

"What are you talking about? That was water!?!" Lorraina stated and questioned simultaneously.

"Where do you think the water comes from?" Richard said over his shoulder as he headed up the stairs, Lorraina following fearfully like a puppy again.

"Then how does it look so clean and taste so good, if it is sewage? Lorraina asked sarcastically.

"Well, there is obviously something that your movies have failed to teach you, that books and experience can."

"So, are you lying just to scare me this time?"

"Actually no... not this time. It is actually cleaned and filtered sewage." Richard responded entering the control/surveillance room now. He turned on a few lights and switches, and got everything up and running. He began looking at all the vantage points from the camera to see if there was any motion.

"There!" he shouted. "Look Lorraina, right there! Their car is there, and Mr. Avera's car is over on the other side. One of them is getting out of the driver's seat of Mr. Avera's car? That's odd." Richard slowed down his speech, wondering with frustration and a furrowed brow, and then rapidly raising one side, inquisitively.

"Is Mr. Avera here?" Lorraina asked fearfully.

"I don't think so, he never comes out here" Richard moved around the room looking at the various cameras. "They didn't sound like they were worried about that when they were talking earlier." He said, zeroing in on a specific scene where the other car was.

Richard could see Captain Cobrin waiting, leaning against a car. He could also see Grady walking toward the captain from Mr. Avera's car. Mr. Avera was nowhere in sight as Richard panned the entire area.

"I bet they are going to try to frame Mr. Avera for killing Krista!" Lorraina began. "Where is Krista, I'm so worried! What if they killed her? What if she's already dead? What if we are too late to stop them? How are we going to stop them?" Lorraina frantically babbled on and on.

"Oh Richard, it's just like Rita in the case of the courthouse and the mystery of the stolen trailer. I don't know what to do!" Lorraina blurted out in a full panic, pacing around the room as she made large motions and dramatic movements with her arms and hands. "Oh what can we do?" she moaned and pulled her hair in a stressed out motion.

"You can be quiet, calm down, and stay focused so that I can think. And for goodness sakes, stop talking about all your movies. Don't you have any real-life experiences?"

"I guess I will once I tell people my best and only friend is dead!" She snapped back defensively.

Zooming in now, with the camera fixed on the scene – looking closely at the car and the men, Richard and Lorraina could scarcely breathe or blink. "Look, that must be your friend that Captain Cobrin is pulling out of the car."

"Krista!! She's alive!" Lorraina yelped. "How can we save her?"

"First, we have to wait and see what they do. If we go down there now, or let them know that we are here, or that you are still alive, then we are all dead."

CHAPTER 13

"Get over here you little sassy brat!" Captain Cobrin began. "You annoy me, and you are hideously ugly... so you win the prize! You girly, you get to die. You'll die nice and slow and utterly alone girly!"

"You know," Grady wanted to add something to the situation. "We enjoy killing, kid," Grady started in, trying to show off for the captain. "It's our favorite pastime, Brownie."

"Brownie?!?" Krista said, agitated. "You know if I'm going to die anyway, then why not keep my sass till the moment I die? Brownie, really, is that all you could come up with? Look, I've been raped, threatened, and bullied by just about every guy and even every boy, since I came to Utopia. So you think I'm sheltered or gonna get my feelings hurt from being called Brownie? Don't you think racism is supposed to be dead by now? I thought it was old school, in your Utopia. I wuz tol' that's the reason for havin' your stupid ol' Utopia. I thought it was over and out? Are you guys old or behind the times?"

"Wow! This girl is more obnoxious than the last one! Too bad the old man is not here and we could just give her to him." Grady rolled his eyes and looked toward the captain.

"What old man? Mr. Avera?" Krista sassed. "He wouldn't kill me; he wouldn't waste his reputation on a pitiful, sassy, colored girl! Do you think I forgot everything from before you tried to brainwash me with Utopia?" Krista yelled, as Jace Cobrin ignored her and tied her hands behind her back slowly to scare her.

She continued to fight verbally, and tried to get away a little, but she recognized that she couldn't outdo them both physically. "I remember downtown streets and gangs and thugs and tramps and people having to survive through selling themselves, so how is Utopia any different, you tell me?" She yelled and glared out in the distance in anger with sweat beginning to form little beadlets upon her face.

"It was 'posed to be a place with new opportunity and everything was said to be 'brand new' on your posters and billboards and in your rule books and everywhere. You said, 'Old rules now are broken. Everything is changed. All becomes brand new.' You said it, you all said it, ya preached it, and teached it, crammed it down our throats, an' I see nothin' brand new! Same ol' perverts, same ol' greed, same ol' rich, white guys. You show me your motto!"

"You asked for it, girl!" Jace got angry and short tempered. "Old things now are broken" he said, kicking her feet out from under her. "Everything is changed' he said aggressively as he dragged her by her foot on her stomach, her chin digging into the cement-like dust and embedding gravel into it. "And the world will be brand new... with you out of it!" He finished, speaking aggressively as Grady opened the gate to one of the outdoor sewage pits.

Jace continued to drag Krista until he got her up to the edge of the septic pit. Grady could see he needed some help and pulled her along, with Jace rolling her up over the retaining ledge of the backfilled dirt.

"Bye, bye, Brownie" Jace said, looking Krista directly in the face down at the ground level. "At least now we don't have to see you anymore, since you match your new background" he said and then began laughing and shoved her over and into the pit.

"Come on Grady, I can't stand this stench any longer, hers or this facility. I'm going to need to shower for a week after this," he said, flies buzzing everywhere, after dusting himself off and walking towards the car.

"Shouldn't we close the gate?" Grady asked Jace.

"Nah, let's see how far she gets, if she can get out of this one." Jace said, after hearing Krista splashing and gagging and trying to breathe in after partially surfacing.

"Let's see if she can even make it to the gate, then we will watch her try and run away. Then she'll get this crap caked and baked onto her muddy skin in this heat. No one would even notice she's dirty, if they were here because she's already filthy, she told us herself." He scoffed shamelessly.

Grady's phone began to play the music from the *Phantom of the Opera* and before it could play more than ten notes, Captain Cobrin's phone was buzzing and alarming as well. "Oh great! We are being summoned." Jace sarcastically mocked.

"We can't just ignore Mr. Avera, Jace." Grady began. "I know that you have a lot of stuff on him, but he's powerful and he's got a lot of friends and loyal followers. They trust..."

Jace cut him off, "It's Captain Cobrin to you Grady, I already told you! We can ignore him, and we will for now, but we do have to get back."

"What about the girl?" Grady worried constantly about being told on, and his family and wife knowing what type of double life he led.

"She's not getting out of there, Grady! Just look at the pitiful swamp monster. She can scarcely keep afloat and has gone under 4 times already. She'll never make it, not in a million years! And anyways, then we can frame someone else, because we would never be this sloppy," he cackled. "Now come on, we gotta get going."

CHAPTER 14

"Stop touching me!" Hayden shouted. "Leave me alone!" he screamed. "Why are you torturing me? Get the naysayers away from me" he wailed and moaned.

"He's been like this for two hours" the nurse exclaimed to the doctor who had just walked into a monitoring room. The room was small and off the side of a detox room in the mental health ward of Hayden's local hospital. The window that they observed him through was like a mirror on the other side so that Hayden could not see them, much like the type used in jails.

They did not consider Hayden a criminal, but had to strap him down to a bed. This was in order to keep him safe, as he had been acting out aggressively toward others and himself. He had also been speaking to people that were not there.

"What do you think happened to him?" The large, muscular, male nurse asked the psychiatrist. "I've had to wrestle him down a few times, as he has broken the Velcro straps that he was placed in twice now. Look, I'm a tough guy and I'm exhausted, he's gotta be on something."

"Has the toxicology report come back yet?" Doctor O'Donnely asked, in a fairly concerned manner.

"No, it hasn't, but it should be back soon, I was told."

"Well... sorry, I didn't catch your name?" the doctor questioned the nurse.

"Jesse Rampton sir, I know I'm not typically on this floor, so I'm not surprised you don't know me, but they needed somebody strong enough to help with this guy. I'm normally working in the PEDs department, uh, I mean Pediatrics department that is." Jesse finished.

"Well, Nurse Rampton. I am very formal and thorough in my department. I recognize that working with scared children is different... but make sure in your time on this unit you use no abbreviations, nicknames, or jargon. I need full notes with details on all records. I want to know the second any data, reports, test results, or anything pertinent comes back. No waiting around to tell me if he is acting strangely – in a new way that is – or breaking anything, etc. I need to know about any new changes immediately." The doctor stopped only for a breath.

"I personally saw this patient two weeks ago

for the third time. I completed my evaluation with him and never saw even a hint, or tinge of this behavior. He was quiet, calm, scared of his own shadow, highly intelligent, obsessed with his work – which was paleontology – and other than that, he was pretty composed. He behaved with what I would call unremarkable behavior. This is completely opposite behavior and this, concerns me. I did just prescribe him with new medication two weeks ago. The medications I prescribed, however, could not possibly have caused these results... not alone, anyways."

"Doctor O'Donnely, Doctor O'Donnely, please call Nurse Benton on line 3. Doctor O'Donnely, Doctor O'Donnely, please pick up line 3." A nurse's voice came through over the doctor's personal voice-alert neckwear.

"This is Dr. O'Donnely" he said, holding down the transmitter on the device, "Go ahead."

"Doctor O'Donnely, we have a female patient, age 57, just checking in from an ambulance with her husband. The paramedics reported that they have never seen any lady of her age so physically strong, feisty, irrational, hallucinating, etc." Nurse Benton began explaining over the hospital intercom system.

"Her husband claims that it's just in this last week or so - the first time in 31 years, that they've been married – that he's ever seen anything like it! There's two male EMTs trying to keep her physically restrained, and safe, but it's almost impossible for them. Our emergency room staff can't continue to handle her safely, and they have reached out to me to check in with you. What do you want us to do?"

"For now, call security in, and we'll make a bed for her up here. I'll be there momentarily."

"Alright, thank you doctor," the nurse responded rapidly.

Doctor Teagan O'Donnely now turned to Jesse, "Nurse Rampton, I obviously have to get over to handling this new arrival, and I think that Mr. Baulmfield needs an 8mg dose of Lorazepam. It should calm him down a little and make him more manageable."

Scooting his medical exam stool across the room after completing some notes, he finished giving directions. "I don't think that it will interact with the prescriptions that I had placed him on. So, as long as he wasn't or isn't on something else, he should be fine. I wanted to wait for the toxicology report, but I think we are in a more emergency situation here and he needs to calm down. He's been revved up, dumping cortisol non-stop for way too long now. I'll be back shortly, I hope."

CHAPTER 15

"Mrs. Hessop, I presume? I am Doctor O'Donnely." He said half-asking, half-stating.

"Mrs. Hessop, I'm not familiar with your case, as I'm sure you know that I am not your doctor. So, I am wondering if you could please catch me up a little on what's been going on with you?" he said, politely and with genuine care.

"Well, if you're not my doctor, than who the heck invited you, four eyes!?" Marilyn Hessop blurted out rudely.

"Ma'am, I am the psychiatrist on call at the hospital tonight, and I am happy to help in any way that I can." The doctor continued, not allowing her demeanor to faze him even slightly.

"Well then go help someone else. I don't want your help or need your help! There's nothing wrong with me, it's my husband who is the problem and everyone else."

"Ok, can you tell me what he's been doing and what everyone else has been doing? What seems to be the problem?"

"Nothing seems to be the problem, Mr. Darby O'Gill. It's just that there are little people trying to steal me to the underworld and then the banshee will come take me. Ha, ha, ha." Mrs. Hessop began snorting.

"Mrs. Hessop!" Doctor O'Donnely said. "I do recognize your joke about the Darby O'Gill movie, but I'm trying to help you and your family. If you don't tell me your version of the situation, I'm going to turn the time over to Mr. Hessop. Is that clear?"

"It's as clear as *The Emperor's New Clothes,* Doc. Ha, ha, ha. What's up, Doc?" Mrs. Hessop began mimicking movies.

"Th-Th-Th-Th-Th-That's all folks," she cackled and croaked like a frog suddenly. "Hey, that's funny! I could be a frog and then I'll have you kiss me and see if you're a prince."

"Ok, your time is up! Mr. Hessop, can you give me some background as to what the main concern is?"

"Ok, ok... the main concern is a little hard to say, Sir" he hesitated briefly, "Other than the obvious that is."

"With your wife in the room? Is that what you mean?"

"Yes Doctor, she gets mighty upset if I talk about her or try to explain."

"Go ahead and try, please. We will help out if things get out of hand," he said, signaling security to step forward a little.

"Ma'am, if you act violently to your husband, yourself, or anyone in this room, you will have to be restrained. We are giving you a fair warning." he finished, turning back to Mr. Hessop. "Now please, go on."

"Well, Doctor, my wife is normally very calm, reserved, peaceful, quiet, kind of boring, I guess. Not to be offensive to her or about her, but she just knits, gardens, goes on walks, sips herbal teas, beads, naps, reads to children at the library, etc. It's a good kind of boring, but she was getting depressed sir, and wanted to see somebody. See somebody to help her with medications to see if she could feel 'alive' again. She got on some anti-depressants or something. They gave her these meds," he said, handing Doctor O'Donnely the bottle. "And life has been changing for the worse pretty much daily since then."

"How so?"

"Well, at first it was just strange dreams that were very vivid and telling her things. Then it was her killing in her dreams and wanting to kill and talking about how exciting the dreams were. Then it was her covering every entry, window, crack, outlet, smoke alarm, and digital device with toilet paper, thinking that the devices were watching her." Mr. Hessop stopped momentarily and looked off to the side toward his wife, knowing she would get angry at him for talking about her.

"Please continue," Dr. O'Donnely prodded.

Hesitating only a bit longer, Mr. Hessop continued. "She thinks that there are literally people behind the outlets, in the walls, in the cracks, in the hinges, and even on the lid of the toilets. She thinks that they are recording her, and using this to poison all people against her so that they can make sure she can never sleep again."

Mr. Hessop continued at a rapid speed. "Normally around this time of year, she is already prepared for Christmas. She has decorated for the holidays even up to a month before, normally. Not this year, though! This year, she broke nearly half of the ornaments! She accidently cut herself on them earlier today, because she squeezed them till they popped. You know, the old fashioned glass ones? Anyhow, she squeezed them, because she said that there were little gremlin devils – who lived in them – who were feeding data to Mr. Avera."

Without scarcely a breath, he continued. "Doctor, she thinks that this little toy elf, that you are supposed to hide in the house, that I have seen in commercials, is really Mr. Avera's 'Eyes'. And, that he designed the tradition to spy on kids and snoop on their parents. She told me, a few days ago, that she thinks that I work for Satan, and..."

"Ok, ok, I hear you Mr. Hessop. That's all I need for now. I appreciate it, this helps."

"Mrs. Hessop, who do you think I work for?" Doctor O'Donnely asked her, in a kind and compassionate manner.

"I hope God, or we are going to be seriously outnumbered!" she said.

"We?" the doctor wondered verbally.

"Yah, me and Tinka here. She is trying to protect me against evil, and she's gonna bark and keep you up all night long, and she's gonna bite you if you touch me. She's the best guard dog ever and she tells me when people are bad. She's been barking at Mr. Hessop all night and day for four days, so that's why I know he's working for the underworld. But you... she hasn't barked at yet, so I'm not sure."

"So Tinka is your dog?" Doctor O'Donnely asked patiently, looking at Mr. Hessop.

"Was our dog, Sir... she's been dead for four years or so," Mr. Hessop responded.

"Ok, well Ma'am, I have many other patients to get to tonight. We are just going to start an IV, and get some fluids and electrolytes pumped into you, maybe give you something to help put you to sleep for a little. I would like to run some blood tests to see how your overall health is, and maybe check why the medications you started aren't working well for you. Does that sound ok?"

"No, it does not sound ok. I'm not letting anyone touch me and neither will Tinka."

"I'm sorry, Ma'am, but because you hurt the paramedic and assaulted the EMT, and pulled a knife on your husband, and have self-harmed, cutting your hands to shreds with your Christmas ornaments, you do not have a choice anymore! We are trying to help you and keep you safe, those are our top priorities – keeping you safe, and others safe. Everyone has to be safe, Mrs. Hessop. We will do our best. I'll come back and check on you shortly!" the doctor said, leaving the room.

As he went out of the room and into the hall, he told the nurse – that he had spoken to earlier, Nurse Benton, to give Mrs. Hessop some Lorazepam. "Also, give some fluids, but first draw for toxicology and CBC, A1C, CRP, and also..." He was interrupted again by the intercom system he wore around his neck.

"Dr. O'Donnely, Dr. O'Donnely, please..." He pressed a button silencing it. He wrote out a bunch of other tests and handed the long list of tests to the nurse, and headed down the hall.

CHAPTER 16

"Mom, Mom, I'm so glad that you are here. I'm so glad you came. I was so sure that I would die before you got here. Oh, Mom!" Hayden said, enthusiastically hugging and picking up his mother and spinning her around, entangling himself in his IV cords, partially. "I'm so, so, so happy you are here so that we can talk about old times, before I die and you can help me plan my funeral."

"Hayden, Hayden, seriously, put me down! I'm glad you are happy to see me. I'm glad I got here. I'm glad you are ok, but you seem plenty healthy and strong, I don't think you are going to die. Not any time soon anyway."

"Mom, you don't understand these things." he said, setting her down, quickly feeling irritated. "I understand stuff like this," he said. Now somber, moody, and unable to regulate his emotions very well, going from elated to discouraged, in seconds, he crawled into the hospital bed – after fixing his IV cords. He situated himself and pulled the blanket up over his head and pouted.

Rocking back and forth a little, he peeked out from the blankets and asked Jesse, the nurse, for a warm blanket. Jesse looked at Hayden's mom, checking with eye contact to see if she felt safe with her son, without him there for protection.

"I'm fine" she said shrugging.

"Do you need anything, Ma'am?" Jesse asked.

"Just some ice water would be great, thank you" she answered. "I always love the crushed ice you have here. At least that is one good thing about the hospital."

"Anything else, Hayden?"

Hayden popped his head out from under the covers. "Yah, some food. I'm starving to death in this prison. Am I allowed to eat yet?"

"I don't know yet, Sir. I have to check with your doctor. I can do that right now though, if you'd like me too?"

"You'd better, or I'm breaking out of here. I'm going to die of starvation! Now get going!" Hayden shouted, as he began wadding up tissue from the tissue box and attempting to throw it at Mr. Rampton, as Jesse was exiting the room.

The door locked behind him, with no doorknob or way out, since this was a room designated for people experiencing mental illness and often dealing with issues of self-harm and aggression, or violently acting out toward staff and others.

"It is a prison, Mom, we need help!"

"Well maybe we should pray. I honestly don't know how to help you right now, son, aside from that. Let's just pray."

"You go ahead, it can't hurt. I doubt it will do much, but it can't hurt and maybe it will make at least one of us feel better."

"I'll say it then, ok?"

"Sure, Mom," said Hayden.

"Dear Lord, we come before thee at this time to ask for help for Hayden. He is very..." Aleta stopped in her tracks. She hadn't really been closing her eyes solidly when she bowed her head, or as she began praying. She was a bit concerned to let her eyes off of Hayden.

Now she could see why, as she observed him pulling a long, dark, strand of hair out of the hospital blanket and eating it. He put it on his tongue like a noodle and began munching happily like a kid with spaghetti and meatballs. Back and forth, from side to side, he swayed and made a humming noise of happiness, like a toddler, as he enjoyed slurping in the hair, winding it in with his tongue.

The prayer was over. She couldn't say another word out loud. Gulping hard to keep from throwing up she turned her head in disgust. Aleta closed her eyes momentarily. Speaking to God in pleading form quietly and under her breath, she said "God, please help him. Give my son back."

"So, Mom, before I die, I want to tell you some things about me."

"Ok Hayden. I'd love to hear, son." she said in a weary, worried tone, pale as a ghost.

"My favorite animal is a cow! I want to be a cow farmer when I grow up."

"I thought it was a Hadrosaurus that you wanted to be when you grew up?"

"No, that was all pretend so no one would make fun of me. I always loved cows and wanted to jump them in races like horses normally do, and maybe someday in the Olympics."

Aleta Baulmfield had no idea how to respond, or if any of this were true, or whether he was still just hallucinating. She wished that there was something that she could do to help him, but she was out of any ideas, and was terribly exhausted and worn down already.

"Oh, and I have always wanted and dreamed of a honey yellow... no actually a banana cream yellow, metallic mini-van. That's the car of my dreams mom. Can you please buy me one?" Aleta knew instantaneously, once he said that, that he was still affected by the medications.

CHAPTER 17

"Now that we're all dry and clean, I need you to tell me some things about yourself: your mom, your family, and such. While we wait out this storm, I need to get as much information from you as I can, so that I can help you."

Bridget continued in a rather rushed manner, "I don't have a landline anymore and my mobile phone is probably toast. I'm not going to get to my mom's house tonight anyway, that's for sure! Thank goodness we set the celebration for my brother's birthday a week early. We did that, so that we could have his party and then get him to somewhere safe before Utopia comes to take him. But this way, I will still get to see him, and maybe they'll reschedule his party, so that I can be there."

"How do you know that they won't get him somewhere safe, before you get there" asked Liam.

"Because I am the one taking him into his hiding place" Bridget quickly responded. "Wow! Ok, look at all this talking from me; I need you to talk now." Bridget said, looking a much brighter, cleaner looking young man in the face now.

"What's a landline?" Liam asked.

"A landline is a phone that is hooked up through a cord to the land. They plug into your wall into a special "phone jack", they used to call it, and then that runs through the house, and then out to a telephone pole.

A telephone pole looks like a power pole, but it is not. It is the kind of phone everyone had till I was born, and now pretty much nobody has them. They are old fashioned and the only places that have them really are old buildings out in rural areas that have no cell towers, and of course a lot of old people have them, because they don't want to learn anything new. This place had a land line still, when I got it, but I didn't want to pay for it. I guess right now it would have been nice if I had. But hey, you are sidetracking me. We are supposed to be talking about you. So, tell me about yourself."

"What am I supposed to say?" Liam began awkwardly.

"When and where were you born? What did your mom do or sell at this shop? Where is she from? Where is your dad from? Did you ever see her with any friends or family or strange people you didn't know? Did you..."

Liam cut her off abruptly. "Ok, that's too many questions for me to remember them all. I need to think for a second."

"I'm sorry, let's start with what you know for sure... like your birthday." Bridget said, now handing Liam a mug of hot chocolate. "I love a nice cup of hot chocolate when I'm cold and my nerves are kinda frozen. Go ahead and drink it and I'll get a notebook to keep track of things." Bridget rummaged around a mess of papers on her desk.

Most things in our home were orderly and comfortable, with an antique Victorian appeal. The room had chair-railing and picture-railing throughout the main area. Traditional hardwood floors had been refinished and antique lamps, vintage wall paper, chairs, furniture, and even a roll top desk. The roll top desk was now wide-open overflowing with uneven, disorderly papers. When Bridget opened an underneath cupboard, more papers and trinkets fell out, onto her fuzzy carpet/rug which matched nothing else in her apartment.

"Grrr, why do these things always have to happen when I don't have time?" She said in a moment of frustration. "Forget it, I'll clean it up later, here's the notebook I was looking for," she exclaimed, rummaging around again for a pen. Liam watched her now in wonder and tried to remember details about his mother that would help him find her. He realized finally, that this kind woman in front of him who was so like his mother, but, yet much younger, and not as wise and even-keeled... was most certainly NOT her.

His eyes went into a slight trance for a moment, staring up at the light. He sipped his hot cocoa, holding it dearly and tightly with both hands, hunched over a little. His body was all wrapped up in a large woolen blanket. He was re-playing his last encounter with his mother in his head and remembering everything, almost in slow-motion.

Pictures of the encounter flashed in his mind, like quick clips from a movie. Her toes, the ocean, the sound, smell, his father, the boardwalk, himself, his clothes, a toy that his mother had given him which had been hers, he saw it all. He recalled that he had dropped it when his dad pulled him toward the truck aggressively.

He had pleaded with his father to go back. He begged for the toy and his father ignored him and told him to "shut up". He remembered his mother's look of pain and sadness after she picked it up out of the sand, brushing it off and waving as they drove away, tears streaming down her cheeks.

"Are you alright?" Bridget interrupted his thoughts and memories. "You look very lost in thought. Looking at the lights will hurt your eyes."

"I was thinking of my mother and that last time I saw her." He paused briefly, for a moment. "If only I had not dropped the toy! I really wish I still had it, or something to remember her by. But then my dad probably would have busted it up or thrown it away by now, anyhow. He's like that, you know." Liam said, looking up at Bridget now, his face intensifying with rage.

"He pretty much never hit me, just dragged me around and shoved me, or smacked me upside the head" he went on. "But he broke, hit, smashed, and destroyed almost everything else." Liam concluded in a forlorn fashion, looking down at his empty mug, as the wind howled and rattled the shutters and roof of the early 1900s boardwalk building.

"So, what are your parents' names, Liam? If I'm going to help you, I need you to give me some information." Bridget said, trying to help Liam snap out of his melancholy mood.

"My dad's name is Howard Heepen. He's pretty old. I don't know how old exactly, but I remember celebrating his 55th birthday before Mom left, so I guess he's probably close to 60 years old."

"What's your mom's name?" Bridget prodded.

"She was always called 'mom'. I never really heard anyone call her anything else, except Dad called her 'Sugar' when he was happy. He called her mean, bad words when he was mad. I'm not one hundred percent sure what her name was, but Grandma always called her Nia (***nee - uh***). I guess I thought it was another language or something."

"Nia!?" Bridget questioned, surprised and kind of loudly. Instantly recalling the incident earlier in the day, when Hayden Baulmfield had called her Tyrnia ***(Teer-nee-uh)***, she was eerily taken aback. She had never met Tyrnia before, and had never heard of anyone being called Nia or Tyrnia. With how strange her day had gone already, and Liam confusing her with his mother – she felt it could be possible for there to be a connection. "Was it Tyrnia by chance, Liam?"

"I'm not sure, but I guess I did find a letter from her once to her brother. It was signed with a TSH and a heart. I knew it was her handwriting, so I always wondered why she signed it that way."

"What was her brother's name?"

"It didn't say. I don't remember any uncles or relatives except Grandma and Grandpa."

"What was your grandma's name?" Bridget inquired, feeling like they were getting nowhere.

"Now that I do know!" Liam responded with enthusiasm. "Grandma was named Wanda, and Grandpa was Walter. They loved that they both had W names, and were excited to always remind me that my name was after them, a W also. They always asked me to go by William, but my mom would correct them and say, 'I want him to be Liam, Mom and Dad.' They were super funny and nice. I miss them."

"What was their last name? Can you remember?" Bridget was curious to see if they were any relation to her, since two people in one day saw a great resemblance in her and someone they knew.

"I remember it began with Z, since they would always say that they were the last on everything, due to their last name. I'm pretty sure it was Zaugg. Oh yah, it was, because it rhymed with hog. That's how my mom taught me to remember it, when I was very little" Liam chuckled a little to himself.

"Of course, they both died... so, I didn't see them after the first few years of my life. They died when I was six years old. They were just sitting on their couch, watching TV and no one ever found out why. I miss them!" Liam looked somberly down to his feet and wiggled them around a bit, as he recalled his past. Bridget just waited for him to speak again.

"We used to have big dinners at their house for holidays, but, on the way home every year mom and dad would fight and dad would holler at my mom." Liam faded off into memories again, tired now and slowing down.

"Liam, did you eat anything today? I can't believe it! How silly of me for not thinking to ask you."

"No ma'am! I'm pretty hungry." He responded weakly.

"Let's get you some food, and we can talk more about this later." Bridget began to get up to go over and get Liam something to eat, but then paused momentarily and turned back and came over to his chair. She crouched down again. "I do have one more question first."

She looked happy and a little excited. "I'm not exactly sure what I'm doing for Christmas yet. But I was wondering, since it's only in 2 days, if you had any plans, or if you'd be willing to share it with me?"

"I thought you were going to your mom's house. I don't think she'll want me there, and she might tell on me and I'd have to go to Utopia."

"Is that the only thing holding you back?" She asked gently, putting her hand on his left forearm.

"Definitely! Of course it's holding me back. I'm scared! I don't ever want to go to that place. My older brothers all got taken and we've pretty much never heard from them since." Liam became panicked.

"Well, my mom would be your best supporter in that regard, kiddo. She despises Utopia and has a secret plot for us to help my little brother Brady to not have to go there. We can include you in the plot, and figure something out."

"But isn't it illegal... she's going to risk going to jail... for me?"

"Not just for you, but for her son too. Besides, it's only illegal because wicked, controlling men made it illegal. Laws are the only thing making something legal or not, and men are the ones who make the laws. My mother and I are much more concerned with what's right or wrong, good or bad, ethical or not – not what is legal or illegal!"

Thinking for a minute of how to word an explanation, and help it to make sense to a young boy, Bridget then continued. "Men and women have been making an awful lot of 'laws' lately that have been extremely wrong. Even for the last ten years or so, they have been finding ways to make things that were once jail-worthy and very illegal (because they were wrong) – now legal, just because they have money and power and want to do those horrid things."

"I'm not sure I really understand," Liam furrowed his eyebrows and squinted, looking quite confused.

"So, what I am trying to say is that when the law is not in the best interest and safety of children and families and good, kind women, and people who are smaller or weaker, so that the biggest bully can't always win, then sometimes we have to stand up and fight back, in any way that we know how, until we can get new laws made which keep people safe and able to be free and find happiness. Does that make any more sense to you?"

"A little more, I guess. Well, not exactly though"

"Well my mom and I believe in God, and I don't know what you believe, but we try to always obey the law, unless it is going against God's laws. You know, laws like 'do not kill', 'do not steal', 'do not covet', and ones like that – or if it is taking away people's freedoms (their ability to make choices themselves and for their young children). Well Liam, Utopia goes against all good and all freedoms! It takes away our rights of 'Life, liberty, and the pursuit of happiness'. There comes a point when average people – or just regular citizens –must stand together and fight for changing the laws for what's best for everyone... not just one group of people, a minority, or elite group who wishes to control, take over, or usurp authority. I know that I'm not doing the best job explaining things. I am not a teacher, I am just trying to help it make sense to you."

Liam's head began to nod off, Bridget noticed. "I can see I'm putting you to sleep," she said tapping him on his arm. "I'm sure you're pretty tired. I'll go get you that food, and you can take a nap. Oh yah, but are you going to join us for Christmas? It would make me very happy."

A smile finally broke across Liam's youthful, slender face displaying his gnarly teeth, "I would love to!"

CHAPTER 18

Faster than anything Lorraina had ever done before, she flew down the stairs and through the corridor and back up the steps to the exit. She plowed through the exit door and raced full speed across the property to Krista. She was easily able to find Krista, now that she had seen a bird's eye view of the sewage treatment facility from the security room.

Richard raced after her also recognizing that the coast was clear, and knowing that time sensitivity was of utmost importance. He was not quite as speedy as Lorraina on the stairs, however, as his age and arthritis made it more challenging for him to get down the steps. He was very physically fit and had an extremely high level of long term endurance, but the shorter burst of speed and energy were behind him now.

As Lorraina reached the site, she gasped at the stench only for a split second and then crawled up the side, reaching her hand and full arm out to Krista. She laid her body on the ground in an attempt to grasp her friend and balance her own body at the same time, so that she would not fall in. Richard wasn't too far behind, and he realized that this method of rescue was not going to work. He had already been plotting before the guards had even left.

So he brought a Rescue Kit from the surveillance room which included rope, alcohol wipes, gauze, emergency eye care, a mouth-to-mouth device, and much more. He hoped not to need all of the items, but planned for the worst. He'd been trained for emergency combat rescue and relief missions in the military and unfortunately had had to use his skills to both kill and save throughout his prior military career.

Pausing to drop the bag near the gate and grab the rope out, along with catching his breath, he tried to determine his next steps. Richard securely tied the rope to the gate posts and walked it out over the edge of the rectangular preliminary sewage treatment pond.

Thinking about too many things at once was causing Richard to be more uneasy and unorganized than Lorraina had yet seen him. He finally handed her part of the rope and said, "Once I tie her onto this rope, pull with everything you've got! She can't reach out to you because she's unconscious."

"She doesn't know how to swim! They never taught us to swim!" Lorraina cried intensely, in a full panic.

"That doesn't matter right now! She's unconscious, passed out. Thankfully she's floating with her face mostly out of the sludge, that's astonishing!"

"It's a miracle! Not just astonishing!" Lorraina interjected.

"We don't have time to debate about beliefs or semantics here. You pray if you want to, but your eyes better be open and you better pull that rope when I say! I gotta go in there now" Richard said, as he plunged straight in, holding onto the rope.

Knowing how to swim, keeping his head above the sludge water, wearing a medical professional's mask – which he had grabbed from the emergency bag – Richard was as prepared as he could be to handle the situation. He made his way toward Krista, who wasn't very far from the side of the 12x24 foot sewage retaining pit.

There were many of these rectangular pits that looked like raised garden beds with dark, rich soil from up in the surveillance room, but were obviously not, when seen up close. They were laid out in rows, 4 deep, 12 wide, all retained within the same gate. Utopia B's waste was all plumbed here and their water came from this facility and about 4 others like it. Those facilities were so large; they almost looked like small cities from an aerial view. This was the smallest of the 5 local facilities and the oldest. It was the original facility from a time before Utopia got out of control in size.

"I've got her", Richard shouted. "She's breathing, but it's weak" he said tying the rope under her arms. "Ok, pull slowly". Nothing happened, so Richard assumed Lorraina hadn't heard him. "Pull!" he hollered again. Still nothing happened.

From a short distance Lorraina appeared to be pulling but nothing was happening. Beginning to struggle with treading to stay afloat in the thick sewage, Richard knew he had to get out soon. He grabbed the rope and began to attempt to pull himself back to land. Doing this, he pulled Lorraina flat on her face and almost into the sludge pit. He felt bad, but didn't have enough energy, ability, or breath to waste on asking questions or apologize at that moment.

He began pulling himself in and was thankful that he had tied one end of the rope off on the gate post. Finally, hurling his human-waste-drenched body over the edge of the pit and back onto solid graveled ground... he began pulling Krista in with ease and speed, ensuring that he pulled in such a way as to keep her head out of the filth.

"I'm sorry I knocked you over" Richard gasped, out of breath, to Lorraina, as he was heaving Krista out of the sewage. "Why didn't you pull?" He asked, in a rather short irritated tone. "Didn't you hear me?"

"I heard you," Lorraina began, as she crawled backward from the edge and wiped the sludge from her hand into the gravel, to get it off the best she could. "I tried!!!" She stated defensively. "I was actually pulling with all my might. I really love my friend Krista. I wanted to save her and I guess I just wasn't strong enough" she began sobbing, pausing briefly, before going on.

"It's too late... now my only friend in the whole world died, because she drowned in poop, my most hateful thing, and I couldn't even help save her! I killed her! It's as if I did it myself." She began a roller-coaster of mood swings and sobbing, yelling, and talking to no-one in particular.

Richard completely tuned her out, not having time for all of the drama and mood fluctuations. He checked Krista's pulse and used many of the items from the emergency bag to wipe off her face, rinse off her eyes, and make sure she was still breathing, continuing to ignore Lorraina's blubbering.

"Why did I never even try to work or lift anything since I got to Utopia? What's wrong with me?? I was so stupid falling for the *'Everything is Changed'* lie. Obviously, people still have to work outside of Utopia, just not those of us inside. How could I have been so blind? If I hadn't been so blind I wouldn't have let my only friend die. How could I have fallen for believing that work was bad for people and that only uneducated people need to work or exercise?"

"You are going to let both of your only friends die right now, and likely yourself, if you don't focus! You really need to stay focused, Lorraina! Just be quiet and help."

"What, I don't understand? I must have missed something."

"Lorraina, your friend is still alive, she's just gotta get some fresh air, and cleaned up. Of course you missed something when you don't pay attention and when you won't stop yapping. She's probably in toxic shock or something. She may have swallowed some of the sewage. We need to get her medical help, but I'm not sure how right now. My wife is a nurse, but first..."

"Uhhhh," groaning noises began coming from Krista, and Richard's comments were cut short. She began seizing and thrashing around a bit. Richard carefully rolled her onto her side and she threw up multiple times in a row. "Where the heck are we?" Krista began.

After wiping her hand across her forehead and then looking at it, realizing that it was covered with sewage, she rolled her eyes and let out a bit of frustration and sarcasm, very consistent with her personality. "Oh... I woke up and went to hell I guess, since you look like an evil swamp-monster-humanoid thing and you're supposed to be dead." She said, speaking to Richard and Lorraina.

"And this ain't heaven! Nothing that smells this gosh awful can possibly be any kind of heaven for nobody." She proclaimed, obviously not too injured, her sass completely unharmed.

Richard grunted a bit of a laugh with a half smirk and then responded. "Being a sewage treatment facility, thankfully they do have a few showers around here. I am sure it is for this exact type of scenario, of falling in. Let's get going now and clean up before I begin puking too!" he said through his mask, not knowing how the girls were even alive with the hideous aroma, with no masks.

"But, how will we take showers with only that pump thing for water? It's too close to the ground to really get under it and there's only a bucket." Lorraina was concerned.

"There are normal showers and bathrooms." Richard responded all nonchalantly.

"Of course Lorraina, why wouldn't they have showers and water here? It's a water treatment facility." Krista said, sitting up now, holding her head and getting dizzy.

Appearing extremely perplexed, Lorraina questioned. "If there are regular bathrooms and there is regular clean water in pipes and faucets in this place, then how come we couldn't use those types of water, instead of that hand pump thing?"

Krista was confused and was standing but seriously staggering.

"Oh yah, about that..." Richard began laughing a little sheepishly. "I forgot about mentioning that. I thought it might be a good life-lesson and a teaching moment at the time, for you to realize that you don't know everything. Maybe I did it to teach you that Utopia kept you guys in the dark on purpose, on some things, so that you wouldn't know how to survive."

"So, another tarantula moment?" Lorraina said angrily. "You think it's just fine to mock me, use my weaknesses against me, and to lie to me if it's going to benefit you or even us. It's still not ok to lie... the ends never justify the means when you are lying," she stated, now quite a ways out of the gate and fenced area and began walking rapidly and angrily toward the building.

"Wait Lorraina!" Krista cried out. "I need help, I don't think I can make it very far," she half-whispered as her strength wore out rapidly.

Lorraina began to walk back and as she passed Richard she glared at him, stuck her nose in the air and squeezed past him through the gate. "I still say you are a liar." She tried to help Krista, but again, she wasn't strong enough. Richard came over and helped on one side of Krista with Lorraina on the other side.

CHAPTER 19

"Why are some people so rude? I think so far you are the only nice man I have ever met." Krista commented and simultaneously inquired of Richard. "I know I haven't known you that long, but I can't think of any man that I personally know who woulda dove into a sewage pit to save me. Then on topa dat, waited outside and hosed off with a freakin' garden hose so that Lorraina and I could have the only two showers here. Why are you doin' dis? Why you even here?" Krista continued, after she and Lorraina were all cleaned up.

All they had for clothes were jump suits that were navy colored, coveralls with small red lettering that read, "*All Becomes Brand New*" in cursive writing and "*Water Works Department*" in all capital lettering, directly below the cursive.

"Well, right now… I am here, or standing in this particular spot, because although I rinsed off with the hose – it's my turn for a real shower – and you happen to be standing right between me and said shower." Richard responded, as his drenched, still fowl-smelling clothes were dripping all over the floor.

"Oh, ha ha, sorry, I din't thinka dat." Krista responded, stepping out of Richard's way so that he could go into the locker room to shower.

"Would you please grab me one of those jumpsuits too? These clothes will never get the stench out."

"Yah, we threw ours in the garbage!" Lorraina piped in.

"Well, that's where these are going!"

"Yah, I'll grab you one," Lorraina said and went to a floor to ceiling cabinet that was filled with stacks of the coveralls, which were organized into sizes. "What size do you wear?" she hollered from around the corner.

"XL, Big and Tall," he raised his voice a little to be heard.

Krista was full of questions. She didn't have much patience and was used to just talking until someone bullied her, pushed her away, or told her rudely to back off. So she really didn't get the hint that Richard wanted some space. "Why aren't you racist?" she blurted out to Richard. "You don't live in Utopia; you just work there, so how did you learn not to be racist? I thought people were only taught anti-racism in Utopia."

"Racism does not stop because we fake that it's not there and proclaim that we're not racist!" Richard answered her partially, as he waited for Lorraina to find the jumpsuit.

"Racism happens because it is taught or demonstrated, and passed on long before age fifteen. It takes, not only new ways of teaching, but good examples of another way of living, a happier, kinder way. Or sometimes it takes experiencing racism against oneself, in an unpleasant manner, before people will change their beliefs and choose to gain compassion."

Pausing to collect his thoughts momentarily, Richard face-palmed out of frustration, then continued in an exasperated tone. "Also, some people don't end up choosing to be compassionate, after experiencing racism for themselves. They often turn around and try to get revenge or 'Pay Back' as some I've known call it. Becoming someone who is not racist or bigoted is not only helped by knowledge and education, but it is a choice." Richard was in teaching mode, having raised many children of his own.

"I don't get it all the way!" Krista blurted out. "I kinda see what yur sayin', but whites never have to deal with racism." She said, just as Lorraina came back into the room. "Yur some other culture... not sure what, but yur not white, so maybe you can understand through experiencin' racism for yurself... but how will whites ever "get it", if they never have to taste it?" Krista continued, fuming with rage and hate from a life full of bottled up feelings, emotions, and experiences that were very fresh, due to her extremely recent racial injustice and despicable treatment.

"Krista, I am half Puerto Rican, and half white. I have most definitely experienced racism in some of the cruelest of ways. But you are dead wrong when you say 'Whites never have to deal with racism'. In some ways, nearly everyone has to deal with racism at some point in their life or another. They have to choose how they handle it, and how they will react" Richard paused and looked at Lorraina knowingly, recognizing the hurt she felt in the background, but not wanting to minimize Krista's pain either.

"Not only do 'White People' have to deal with racism, like every 'People' of every color or combination of colors... but even just calling them 'Whites', is racism. We can't stop racism till we stop classifying people, and grouping them into categories, trying to 'pit' everybody against one another." Richard shook his head in passionate frustration, closing his eyes momentarily, and then lifting his neck and head high to the ceiling and drawing in a deep breath, trying to think of how to help.

"We've had Pro-Utopians and Anti-Utopians, mask wearers and non-mask wearers, vaccinators and anti-vaxxers, pro-life and pro-choice, Republicans and Democrats, rich and poor, and just about every other opposite way of thinking that anyone ever could have, on any various subjects in the world, or even the universe... for crying out loud!" Richard had sped up his speaking, his voice now elevated and riddled with inflections.

"Krista, they actually do have some real racism towards "them" as well, but that isn't the point. It is absolutely NOT a contest!" Richard fidgeted trying not to drip too much more water on the ground, and grabbed a towel off of a shelf, and dropped it at his feet to soak up the sludge water he'd been dripping.

"Look, I'm not an expert or anything and I may not be explaining this very well. My wife is "White", and so are her family, many of our friends, my father, and his side of the family – and I have heard a lot about these racism issues from those friends and family. I have also heard about it from friends of all cultures and races. One of the biggest complaints that I have both seen for myself – and heard repeated – is the fact that ALL peoples, of ALL colors are quite often 'paying' for someone else's racism, not their own," Richard continued, as he used his foot to mop up the floor a bit.

"People are fueled, full of hate, rage, jabs, mistrust, and fear... and then are turning around and acting with racism to each other, because some other person from some other race/culture/group/belief-system hurt them... when they did nothing personally that was racist or mean, and are not a racist person themselves."

"Yur right, yur not esplainin' very well"

"What I am trying to say, is that we've got dozens and hundreds, and thousands of people in this world who feel that they have been racially discriminated against. So, they want to lash out at someone that is from the same race or group of people who hurt them. This is literally as dumb as getting mad that someone's dog bit your toddler, so instead of trying to resolve the issues with the family, who belongs to that dog, you now go get a stick and beat every dog you see for the rest of your life."

"You're calling us dogs?" Krista yelled defensively.

"Krista!" Richard interrupted loudly, "Who said that I classified which group to be the humans, and which group were the dogs? It could have been the other way around. You are simply on the defensive and jumping to conclusions. You want to stay mad and allow yourself to be driven by hate, not hearing me out." Richard stopped briefly.

"How can you blame me, after what those filthy 'white trash' sickos did to me?"

"Krista, breathe..." Richard paused, demonstrating breathing deeply. "Call them sickos, that is surely what they are – but why bring up that they were white? Why does that part matter, unless you were giving the police a description? If they had been black, would you have brought that up?"

"I don't know... probably not. But I hate them!" Krista screamed and clenched her jaw and punched her fist down by her side and stomped on the floor simultaneously.

"What color was the girl who raced to your side and did her best to save you?"

"Lorraina tried to save me? I thought you were the one who saved me," Krista said, not at all considering how Lorraina might be feeling with all of this.

"No amount of revenge, payback, or unforgiving actions will mend your pain or our world. It will certainly never stop racism dead in its tracks!" he said emphatically. "I want to share with you a lengthy piece, which I memorized a really long time ago, back in my school days. It was given by none other than the Reverend Martin Luther King, Jr.

"Let me say as I've always said, and I will always continue to say, that riots are socially destructive and self-defeating. I'm still convinced that nonviolence is the most potent weapon available to oppressed people in their struggle for freedom and justice. I feel that violence will only create more social problems than they will solve... So I will continue to condemn riots, and continue to say to my brothers and sisters that this is not the way. And continue to affirm that there is another way."

Richard continued, with very little breath, "Many people have been mistreated, and accused of atrocities that their grandparents or even further distant relations did, or not even their relatives at all. In fact many of the individuals targeted, actually immigrated over from Sweden, Holland, and many other countries well after slavery was already abolished. And even if their ancestors had owned slaves, or were mean to anyone from any culture... they are NOT their great, great, great, great grandparents."

Krista rolled her eyes and seemed irritated that she had to listen for so long. Richard noticed, but continued, "I don't assume you'd like to be judged for your parents or grandparents, or great grandparents' choices?" Richard finished his speech, looking at Krista in a questioning way.

"Of course not, my dad is a horrible human being. My mom's not many steps above him, my grandparents are pretty chill, but my great-grandpa was a murderer, so I get your point sorta... but 'whites' never have to feel the pain of racial slurs and name calling and stuff. They never..."

Richard cut her off. "Look at your 'supposed' friend here, Krista! Look at her, her head is down, she's cowering a little, and she's not sure what to say or do. She hurts for you; she did everything she could to save you. She was ashamed of herself that she could not save you on her own... and here you are complaining about 'her people' and lumping her and those despicable men together as one group, as if she was part of this. You are 'name-calling' her, when you use 'whites' as a horrible, derogatory thing to be. She is experiencing racism right now, right from your own lips."

"She's never had to endure the stuff that I have had to Richard. I've known her a long time. She doesn't have a clue what it is like to be me!"

"And you don't have a clue what it is like to be her!" Richard hollered back. "Maybe she has not experienced racism to the extent that you have, so you feel justified giving her a taste of someone else's poisoned medicine which they gave you, not a taste of her own medicine! Those were not her actions!"

Richard gathered up the things in his arms a little better to keep them from falling. "Krista, racism stops with each of us making a choice. A choice, that no matter how badly we were hurt by someone else, regardless of race, or culture... we will not hurt people back, save for self-defense or self-preservation, only to keep our rights, liberties, and the freedom to pursue happiness, through religion or whatever means we choose. Happiness is not a right, it's a choice."

"I don't understand everything you're saying" Krista started again. "I just don't think that you or anyone understands me. None of you have had to go through what I've..."

"Stop! Honestly, Krista, you don't know what you're talking about. You don't know what everyone else has gone through. 'Comparison is the thief of Joy' that's a quote by Theodore Roosevelt. And 'Gratitude is the "Key" to joy' and that is a quote from a friend of mine. She is an author named Esther Smith, and she used to teach that to her children all of the time, and talk about it in church. Krista, healing from racism takes a dang lot of time! It takes years of counseling and education and a choice to be kind and forgive and let go of hate. I can't solve one of the world's biggest problems all by myself, while I'm drenched in poop-water, raining a puddle of sludge and filth on the floor."

Walking into the locker-room, Krista attempted to follow him, to continue the debate. Richard continued, "Experts haven't been able to eliminate this issue over the entire course of human history. All I'm saying is that there are 'white people' who have been slaves too, they have experienced pain too. They have feelings too, and they are not all bad! Don't hate people and want to take your anger out on people who didn't hurt you. This woman standing over there, she loves you and did her best to save you... and she calls you her 'Best Friend'. You gotta learn to be grateful." Richard paused very briefly.

"Darkness cannot drive out darkness; only light can do that. Hate cannot drive out hate; only love can do that." Richard quoted. "That was MLK again," he said. "And I don't know what the heck Utopia teaches about personal space, or if such a thing even exists there, but I want a shower and some personal space. So, get out!"

"I just have one more question," Krista insisted.

"I'm shutting the door now," Richard said, kind of plowing her out of the room with the door slowly.

"Another favorite quote from a person I admire," Richard started to say, as he was trying to shut the door without hurting Krista. "When he was asked how we can get rid of racism during multiple interviews... he said, 'Stop talking about it!' His name was Morgan Freeman. He's a great actor, and I intend to take his advice right now!" Richard concluded abruptly, with a final shove of his body, shutting the door till it latched and he locked it.

"When were 'white people' slaves?" Krista yelled through the door. "Seriously, when has any white person ever been a slave?"

Richard was utterly annoyed now, as he had tried so hard to be patient. Had he not already raised seven children with his wife, he surely could not have tolerated it. He felt just as if he had young teenage daughters again, who seemed around the age of thirteen to fifteen, even though these were women in their 20s.

Rolling his eyes, he hollered through the door, "Google it!" Then, he turned on some classical music, full blast, in the bathroom behind the locked the door – in the exquisitely decked out sauna/shower/locker room, that was set up like a millionaire's 'man cave'.

CHAPTER 20

"He was eating a hair off of the bed, Doctor!" Mrs. Aleta Baulmfield insisted to the doctor, telling him of the irregularity and oddness of this action. "This is not normal; you do not know my son. He has autism, and sensory issues, and would normally rather die than eat a hair. He won't even eat food that someone has leaned over, or food that has touched other foods on his plate, or if he deems the food not sanitary enough for any reason. He is not just pulling a prank on me."

"Ma'am," Doctor O'Donnely began asking questions outside of Hayden's room, "Does your son live at your residence?"

"No sir! Although, he does stay over a lot to hang out, wash his laundry, have someone to talk with, or bounce things off of, etc. He probably stays at our house about one to three days a week. The longest he's gone without staying over is 2 ½ weeks. We almost got worried that time. Why do you ask?" Aleta paused and looked curious.

"Does anyone else live near or with Hayden on this frequent of a basis?" He questioned, completely ignoring her question.

"I don't understand."

"Does anyone else, besides you, live in your house? Does anyone live with him in his place?" The doctor prodded for more information.

"Yes, my husband and our two cats live in my house with me, and he lives in his own place. I have no idea if he has friends that stay at his apartment; although I have never seen any evidence of that, when we go over."

Dr. O'Donnely breathed out his frustration and shook his head. "No, no, I don't mean friends or peers his age, per se, Mrs. Baulmfield. I mean are there other relations, relatives? Do you have a sister, or does your husband have a sister, or maybe a grandma, or cousin in her 50s or possibly some type of genetic relative, that lives around here, by chance?"

"I really don't understand, Doctor? What would that have to do with anything?" Aleta was visibly exasperated now. "I really don't see why that has any bearing on my son's recovery."

"Has he given you the Medical Power of Attorney, or do you have an Advanced Directive for him?" The doctor continued to question.

"As a matter of fact, he has. Hayden had signed and notarized all of the paperwork for that, back when he was 18, quite a few years ago." Aleta paused again, "I still don't get it, Doctor, why are you asking?"

"There is a woman in here, at the hospital. She came in not too long after Hayden, and she is presenting with almost identical reactions to medications and from the research conclusions, that I have been leaning towards, it's pretty much an unheard of coincidence, without the two of them being genetically related."

"Well, I don't have any siblings, my husband has three relatives here, but none of them are women."

"So you have no idea of who this woman could be?"

"Well, what's her name?"

"For confidentiality reasons I am not able to give you that information. I wasn't even supposed to tell you that much!"

"Well, I guess it wouldn't matter anyway, I don't really know her name, so that would be of no help. But it could be Hayden's bio mom. We adopted Hayden at birth, but it was a closed adoption, so they never gave her our contact info or names, and they never gave us hers. We are not sure where she lives, but we have never moved and have been in this area since we adopted him over 30 years ago. She could have stayed in the area too. She would be around 60, I think, so I guess the woman could be her."

"Hayden is in no condition to make medical decisions currently. So, do we have your permission to run some blood tests and do some DNA testing?" Dr. O'Donnely began. "We will have to let the other patient know this, and will have to ask her if she is interested in, or willing to do the testing also. I will make sure that she is willing, before putting your son through anything unnecessary."

"However, I do still need some blood work from him, regardless, to check a few things. I'll send the phlebotomist in as soon as I can, and if the other patient agrees, than we will have someone come in to do the saliva swab separately. It may be annoying, to someone with Autism, or 'sensory issues', or to someone who is hallucinating... but it is truly painless." He concluded, slowly vanishing down the hall.

CHAPTER 21

"Mrs. Hessop, I'm finally back. Sorry about the very late promise of coming to check up on you. I've been swamped tonight. It sounds like you sure are having a rough time with this stay. Mrs. Hessop, do you have any children?"

"Why do you ask, Doctor?" Mr. Hessop asked.

"None of your business!" Mrs. Hessop snapped. "Do you have any children, Dr. Doolittle?" Mrs. Hessop cackled and tried to stand up onto one of the soft, teal, padded chairs in the room. She slipped, falling a little onto her husband's shoulder, and knocking him back a bit. This caused the rolling food tray, which was free of food, to shoot across the room crashing into the monitors and hoses and such.

"Mrs. Hessop!" The doctor rose his voice a little, "You almost hurt yourself and others. Please stay off of the furniture and remain on solid ground."

"Does that mean I can't get in my bed?" Marilyn Hessop stuck out a pouting lip right toward the doctor's face.

"You may certainly get in your bed, and may use any furniture as it is intended to be used. In fact, I think your bed would be a great place for you," the doctor said, as he observed Marilyn, now leaning forward and dangling her hair down to the floor. She began walking herself around an imaginary spot, as if it were the center of a circle.

Marilyn stopped for a second and then looked up at the doctor. "Yah, sure I got a kid, a son." Then she began sweeping her hair back and forth on the floor.

"Ma'am please... that's extremely unsanitary!" A short-tempered nurse, with a very commanding personality, barked at Mrs. Hessop, snapping her fingers at Marilyn, observing the scene upon walking into the room.

"What in the world are you doing?" She authoritatively demanded an answer from Marilyn, without yet seeing the doctor in the room. She couldn't really see him as he was standing around the corner, behind the wall where the bathroom area was located. Nurse Benton was very annoyed with Mrs. Hessop, and had no remorse for demonstrating her irritation with her patient.

"I see your demeanor and attitude hasn't changed at all! You're still a lunatic; I should have known they'd stick me with you all night. You better shape up and do everything I say or I will see to it that you are very sorry... you hear me, Ma'am?"

"I don't have to listen to you at all, you're not my doctor!" Marilyn said, still in a pouty, moody manner - very drastically different from her earlier disposition.

"You'll do whatever I say, or I will make your life miserable and a lot shorter!" Nurse Benton was about the same age as Mrs. Hessop. She had maroon colored hair that faded into purple. It was cut mostly short to just below her ear, and that same length along the back of the neck, curling under ever so slightly around most of her head. This was the case, except that her hair was about three inches longer in the front than the back.

Marilyn was ignoring Nurse Benton and continuing to mop the floor with her hair, whipping her hair back and forth from side to side. The nurse's blood pressure was elevating rapidly. "When the doctor is in here... he's in charge. When he's not in here, I am in charge. I am your God for all intents and purposes and if you don't listen to me now..." She lost patience and marched over grabbing Marilyn Hessop's arm and hospital gown sleeve at the shoulder, trying to aggressively jerk her up to force her to listen. The nurse's eyes now met Dr. O'Donnely's. Nurse Benton's escalation of behavior had changed so rapidly that neither Mr. Hessop nor the doctor had really even had time to register or think of how to respond until now. They were kind of frozen in shock, witnessing her behavior.

"Well, I am in here! And I am in charge" Dr. O'Donnely calmly stated, as he stood up straight and tall. "And you will exit this room immediately and never return to it! You will wait at the nurse's station for me, after you apologize profusely, for your behavior, to Mrs. Hessop." He stood holding his clipboard and looking over the top of his glasses authoritatively at Nurse Benton.

"She doesn't even understand anything, she's a retard and you know it! That is why she's on our unit. No one comes to this unit without being one. She won't even know the difference!" She stomped her foot defiantly. "I refuse to apologize to this imbecilic woman. She's one of the most irritating we've had yet. I've had to clean up multiple messes she's made, help her to the bathroom with multiple accidents, and with throwing up, and all kinds of other things. She's very annoying and not at all easy to tolerate or handle. You're not the one who is always in here with the patients. You come in, blab your little opinion, demand for us to do whatever you want, and we have to do all the actual work!"

Dr. O'Donnely calmly tried to ignore much of the trivial, but intentional, jabs she was targeting at him, and to only focus on facts and the necessary things that needed to be said. "Not any different than what you signed up to do, when you chose this career. All nurses know that when they work in a hospital helping patients who are ill, they are going to have messes to clean up and people who are temporarily unstable to work with, especially when they accept a position in this department. Regardless, if you refuse to apologize, then just leave this room at once! We will discuss momentarily – at the front nurse's desk – the consequences of your behavior."

The nurse spun around and pulled off her blue, non-latex, gloves and threw them onto the floor and exited, in a major huff.

"I am appalled at this nurse's conduct. I can assure you, that I have never witnessed that type of behavior on my unit and I will never tolerate it again. If anything like that ever happens again without me being witness to it, please let a head supervisor or myself know at once. It will never happen again from this nurse at this hospital as long as I am here. I will be letting her go as an employee at this hospital immediately!"

"Thank you, Doctor, we didn't mean to be such a bother. I'm so sorry about..."

"No, don't apologize for any of this. It was not your fault or your wife's. This is exactly what a hospital is for, those who are ill and need assistance. The behavior of Nurse Benton is far from acceptable, and I want you to know that I and the hospital do not condone her behavior in any way at all! I am appalled!"

Marilyn had gone into the bathroom and slammed the door by this time. Worried about her safety, the doctor knocked on the door. There was no answer. Flushing of the toilet was heard multiple times already and now again flushing was heard. "I'm going to have to open the door, Marilyn, if you don't respond. We are concerned about you!"

The door flew open, almost hitting the doctor in the face. He stepped back a bit and watched her drag her IV pole out, and walk past him without responding. Her hair was now mostly wet and the shoulders of the hospital gown were wet from her hair.

"I will send a liaison in here and you are certainly always able to file a grievance or call the police and press charges. You have the right to press charges against Nurse Benton for threatening you and grabbing you, especially when you were not at risk of self-harm or potentially harming someone else. You have my utmost apology." The doctor profusely apologized to both of the Hessops. "I need to go handle this and I'll be back shortly." The doctor said, exiting the room rapidly.

Mr. James Hessop quickly followed him and gently shut the door behind him. "Doctor, can you wait up a second? Thank you for standing up for my wife and me, even though my wife is acting crazy right now, she really isn't normally like this."

"It wouldn't matter, even if she was normally like this Mr. Hessop. I have some patients who are always like this... they just didn't have such a sudden onset. Even if a person is mentally-challenged, handicapped, or dealing with mental retardation, there is never a place for shaming, mocking, name calling, controlling, threatening, and yanking people around, or acting without compassion or feeling."

"There are times when, in order to keep a patient safe, we have to act quickly and may even accidently be little rougher than we would like, but it should never be out of anger, spite, revenge, irritation, frustration, or anything like unto it. My staff knows this; I drill it into all of them at our regular meetings. Her actions were unacceptable, and I will never tolerate that behavior here from a hospital staff member. Again, Mr. Hessop, you have my deepest apology."

Dr. O'Donnely looked at his watch and noted something on his clip board. "I believe you when you say your wife wasn't always like this. Some people are, though, and it still would never be ok to disrespect them. Nobody wants to be like this, most people don't even realize that they are abnormal. It is still always my job, even if they personally don't realize that they are affected by mental illness, or are not safe, or are not at their healthiest, to find a solution and remedy. My main priorities are safety and stabilization. I really have to go handle Nurse Benton though, and check in on my other patients. I'll be back shortly."

"Wait, Doctor! The reason I actually came out... well, I mean I appreciate what you are saying and all, but what I'm trying to say is, Mrs. Hessop doesn't have a son, we were never able to carry a child to full term. She miscarried multiple times. She gets very emotional about it and I'm just letting you know, in case it makes a difference or helps. She is so irrational right now, that she's probably just saying that, because you suggested it." James concluded.

"Sir, how long have you and your wife been married?" The doctor wanted to know.

"Sir, 31 years, why do you ask?"

"Well, is it possible that your wife may have had a child without you?" the doctor asked carefully.

"She was never married before, Doctor."

"No offense, Mr. Hessop, but many women give birth without being married."

"But she would have told me, she told me that I was her first love."

"Mr. Hessop, I don't want to cause problems and pain where it doesn't need to be. But it's kind of important. You see, we have a male patient age 33, who checked in shortly before your wife, presenting almost identically in behavior. They are both on the same medication, prescribed by two different doctors around the same time, both from the same pharmacy. But I have other clients on this medication with no reactions."

Doctor O'Donnely took a deep breath, "Both your wife and this patient are now reacting similarly to the medication that I just prescribed to both of them. It is called Lorazepam, which is supposed to calm them down. This reaction has shown up in one study, in approximately .004% of people. They can react in this negative manner, and it can cause them to forget even up to four days of their life. It is rare, so I was unaware of it, until discussing with colleagues about my other patient. Then this happened with your wife."

"So, why does it matter if my wife has a son?"

"Well, the reaction to the two medications might – it appears to me anyway – be a genetic component that triggers this behavior. I have a lot of questions, and a lot more to look into, however the mother of the 33 year old has explained that he was adopted. She states that she adopted him at birth from a single mother in this area in a closed adoption. I am not 100% sure of anything. I am not saying that he is your wife's, but it would help explain a lot. It would help us find some answers, and the only way to find out for sure if he is her son is to do a maternity test. It's painless, just a little swab in the mouth to get some DNA. Then we would know for sure and be able to rule things out."

"I guess I'll ask her about it. I don't know why she would lie to me, though" James said, with his head down in a somber look of uncertainty and shock.

The doctor said, "It's not the right time for that conversation James" patting his shoulder. "It's painful for you right now, but I imagine that it was so painful for her, that that is possibly why she never told you. Good women don't often hide things like this from a good caring man, unless there is a strong reason. I'm not excusing it, just explaining. And it was before you married. So she was not cheating on you. It had nothing to do with you. You were still her 'first love' more than likely.

Many women did not love the men who made them a mother – not because they were uncaring, but because the man was, or they were forced."

"I'll try to just not think about it, I guess."

"Anyhow, I know it's hard, and we can help you seek a counselor about it if you'd like, later on. But for now, we need some immediate answers, as soon as possible! I absolutely need to talk to Nurse Benton."

The doctor turned to walk away. "Remember, Mr. Hessop, it's not the right time, and she's not in the right frame of mind for this conversation. Please wait and everyone will be a lot happier."

James Hessop went back into the room, realizing that they had both left his wife a little too long, with her most recent behavior. Upon entering the room she was talking to herself, or rather to her dog, Tinka, as she imagined.

"They are going to pay, aren't they Tinka? You and I are a great team, we'll see to it that that woman never will want to be a nurse again, we'll..."

James cut her off, "Honey, why is your hair wet? I just realized that your hair and clothes are wet. I remember now that your hair was wet when you came out of the bathroom, right before I went out to talk to the doctor. How did it get wet? Did you pour a cup of water on yourself or something?"

"I took a shower to rinse off. I only washed my hair, because of all of these cords."

"Honey, there is no shower in this bathroom" James said, half asking and half making a statement. He walked over and looked in to make sure he remembered correctly.

"I know that James, that is why I washed it in the toilet! That was my only option, since that lady said it was 'extremely unsanitary' for me to touch my hair to the floor. I didn't want to get SARS or COVID or anything."

CHAPTER 22

"Krista, Lorraina, do either of you know how to drive?" Richard asked. They cleaned up, attempting to cover their tracks by mopping up the bathrooms, emptying the trash, gathering up all their dirty towels and clothes in order to make it look as if they had never been there before. As they were doing this, they found some water bottles in the fridge and took some for the trip.

"Ummm," Lorraina hesitated. "No, not really, I'll warn you that your favorite comment is coming, Richard... I learned a little from watching another movie. But what were we supposed to do? They pretty much restricted us from doing anything but watching movies!" Lorraina responded. "Nearly everything we got to do, was virtual."

"Yah, it's the gospel truth Richard! They don't ever let us drive! Not even let us have a car on the premises, let alone to drive it! I mean, I gotsta agree with my bestie, Lorraina, on this one. We could probably figya it out, cuz we done see 50 plus movies about it and car chase scenes, but we never exacly tried it out for our self, ya know?"

"So, I guess I need to have you try it out on Mr. Avara's car and see if you can do this. Let's see what you got!"

"REALLY?" Krista responded as she jumped up and down for joy and hand-flapped a little, actually squealing a tad. Lorraina was excited with a large smile from ear to ear, but also felt quite a bit of anxiety.

"Wow, what a day!" Lorraina said, a little dismayed. "We really are going to have some adventures to tell our families about when we find them eventually, and our kids someday..." She paused a little. "They're never going to believe everything we've been through" she continued, off in space a little, wondering about her family. "But I must admit, Richard, I'm a little nervous, and what if I ruin Mr. Avara's car?"

"Well, we can wear rubber gloves," he pulled some out of his jumpsuit pocket, "And no one will find our prints. However, those guards were already trying to frame Mr. Avara anyways, so no-one will know it was you. Why would they suspect that? You are both dead, as far as they are concerned."

"But why can't you drive?" Krista blurted out boldly.

"Because I have to go back and pick up my car or they will eventually get concerned and come after me. I need you guys to drop me close, and then flee to my house and meet my wife. She's going to be surprised, but she'll get over it, she's a good lady. Then I will show up as soon as I can. We need to get to this drivers ed. class now" Richard paused briefly.

"Who's first?" He asked, opening the driver's seat door and motioning to the seat with his right hand.

"Me, me, me!" Krista proclaimed excitedly again, "I can't wait ta learn how ta drive!"

"I should've guessed! Ok, Lorraina you are in back, I'm shotgun, and you," Richard said, speaking to Krista, "Need to wait for some instruction." Richard finished authoritatively, getting into the passenger seat and buckling up. "Oh yah, buckle up gals," he said, patronizingly.

"Done!" Krista shouted, "I HAVE driven in a car before, I just haven't been the driver, ya know. I do remember how ta wear a seat belt."

Richard began his instructions, "Ok, so what you need to do is, first..."

"Turn the car on!" Krista chopped him off with her words, in a sassy mimicking tone of voice, with the loud sound of Mr. Avera's souped-up, silver, sports car starting in the background.

"Yes, there's that and then, push the brake to the floor."

The engine revved as Krista accidentally pushed the gas pedal all the way to the floor instead of the brake.

"Not that one!" Richard hollered over the engine noise. "Push the one in the middle." Krista let off of the gas and pushed the brake to the floor.

"Now this time, please listen to the entire directions, before trying anything out. I will tell you when to start." Richard took a deep breath and tried to loosen up as he was completely tense thinking about teaching these child-like women how to drive.

It had been a little different with his teenagers, not much, but it just felt so strange thinking of these adults, who never learned much of anything and were not really able to be independent adults yet, needing driving lessons.

They were frozen in time, sort of, stuck at the age of their traumatic separation from their families. How sad he felt for them, and for their parents who never got to have these unforgettable memories together, as he had gotten to experience with his children.

He could tell how much they were both looking up to him as a father figure and felt a welling up of anger and hate for Mr. Avera and the founders and guards of Utopia. He pushed it away and tried to remember how to teach "kids" how to drive.

"So, when I say... you will continue to push on the brake. Then, you will put the car in reverse, if you need to go backward, and drive if you need to go forward. This little R, stands for reverse or backwards, and this letter D, stands for drive or forward."

"Why can't they just make it simple and have B for backwards and F for forwards?" Krista said impatiently, "Why do they have to make everything so complicated?"

Richard rolled his eyes. "It's not complicated at all, just listen please. Stay focused!"

"It's totally complicated! You're just used to it, and so you don't think so. I mean having to push one lever down with your foot and memorize little letters that don't even start with what they stand for and stuff, and there's more to it than this, still, that I can tell you haven't told me. So, that's complicated!"

"No, you guys just have the attention span of a bug, this is what happens when the world pushes instant gratification and immediate results on everyone, through digital technology, and never makes anyone listen, wait, or let them be bored. Then they never have time to be inventive, patient, or creative." Richard was irritated.

"I think I'm going to become religious like my wife, right about now" Richard said, sarcastically. I'm thinking I need heavenly help and might need to start praying just to survive."

"I'll pray for us!" Lorraina piped in from the back seat. "I'm religious! At least I've been reactivated, now that Krista is going to start driving."

"Go ahead; we could use all the help we can get right now," Richard said, burying his face in his hands.

Krista pushed the brake in and put the car in reverse. Without waiting for further instructions, she let go of the brake. Richard felt the car begin to roll a little. He looked up quickly and said "Wait I'm not ready for you to push the gas yet. You need more directions..."

He was cut off by the throttle of the engine and being thrust forward by the inertia of the vehicle's rapid momentum as Krista put on the gas full force. Thankfully, there was not much behind the car, other than a few large trash dumpster bins, sage brush, and desert, because otherwise they surely would have crashed.

"Push the brake! Push the brake!" Richard yelled. Slamming backward when Krista finally pushed the brake-pedal to the floor, Richard reached over and shut off the vehicle. "That's it, your turn is over! You're going to have to pay somebody to risk their life, to teach you to drive. It's not my responsibility! I care about helping you, but not enough to put all of our lives, in unnecessary danger of death!"

"Oh, c'mon! That was totally awesome! It was like a roller coaster or fair ride." Krista exclaimed after regaining her bearings, from steering all over the place, to avoid hitting the dumpsters. She looked back at Lorraina, "Don't you think that was fun?"

"Not particularly! I actually feel pretty nauseous." Lorraina responded, holding her stomach. "And it was nothing like a roller coaster! They go up and down, not side to side."

"Don't you wanna try?" Krista asked.

"Not really! I'm a little afraid now."

"Don't be afraid!" Richard tried to calm his – and Lorraina's – nerves down, a little. "You just need to take things slower! Don't put so much pressure and force on the car and the pedals. Your actions should be smoother, not so jerky and un-coordinated. It takes time to learn, but don't let one scary situation ruin your outlook for your future of driving."

"Yah Lorraina, I'm not a bit afraid!" Krista bellowed out with glee. "I wanna try again!"

"That's just what I'm afraid of!" Richard darted a stern look at Krista. "It's not good to never drive again, because of one scary incident, but it's the other extreme to not be afraid or cautious at all, after causing a scary incident!" He opened his car door, and then he walked around to her side of the car, and opened the door.

"Now get out! I'm going to show you guys how to drive." Krista got out – and before Richard got in – he asked Krista to switch places with Lorraina, so that Lorraina could have a turn to be taught, and watch closer. Richard covered all of the steps slowly, smoothly, and calmly making sure to remind them, not to rush, or to jerk the car, and to not just forget the steps. He boringly repeated steps again and again. Then he reminded and verbalized each step he was taking, a couple of times over, until Krista became annoyed.

"Seriously, we get it!" Krista interrupted. "Can't Lorraina have a turn now? I'm ready to get out of here."

By that point, Lorraina was calm and ready to take a turn. Richard and Lorraina got out of the car and swapped sides of the car. Before Lorraina got in the car, she was curious which direction she was going to drive. "I feel pretty sure I can do this now, but I just want to get my bearings," she stated. "So which way is south, and north and all of that? Which way are we going to be going? I feel a little overwhelmed about my next step."

She stood, looking out in the distance outside of the car, with her hand over her eyes to shade the sun that was about to set. Shining brilliantly and refracting astounding hues of lavender, neon red, passion-fruit pink, fading into fuchsia, scattering into sunflower yellow, and even a deep blood red, the sky was a beauty to behold, especially on such a challenging day.

"It's going to get dark soon, and I'm pretty sure that I could get you back to Utopia, because I just walked from there and remember it... there's not much to it. However, I've never been to Phoenix, let alone ever driven in a big city, or at all, for that matter. To remember everything about driving, then every direction to your home, and then meet someone new, who might shoot at us thinking we're robbers, it is just too much for me! On top of all of that, there will be flashing lights in the dark, and then city driving... I just don't think it's possible for anyone, their first-time driving, let alone me. I'm not brave about this kind of stuff." Lorraina concluded very hesitantly, in a panic, with her heart racing.

"Look, Lorraina, I see what you're saying. But let's just see if you can even drive first... ok?"

"Ok," she said, looking as if all the color had fled from her veins and body. She sat down, inside; her hands still a bit shaky. She shut the door slowly. She stared at the steering wheel, and then bowed her head and offered a silent prayer. She felt very obligated to figure this out and make it work. She knew that she wasn't physically strong, but maybe she could do this to help out.

Lorraina opened her eyes from her prayer, with a newfound confidence. She was determined and duty driven. She turned on the car, she pushed the brake, and she put the car in drive. She slowly let off the brake and smoothly and slowly pushed the gas pedal. She lightly gave it some more gas and began to drive, copying exactly what she had observed Richard doing.

"You're doin' it!" Krista hollered, excitedly.

"Please not so loud!" Richard motioned to Krista to lower her voice.

"You are doing well. Now let's drive around the building a couple of times to get used to it. Just turn the steering-wheel a little more consistently and smoothly, not such drastic movements. Steadier..." he continued directing, "Now increase your speed a little, slowly, so that you can get used to going faster" he continued.

Lorraina gradually increased speed till she was going relatively fast. "Now Lorraina, when you are ready to slow back down, just make sure that you gradually let off the gas and then slowly and cohesively apply the brakes until the car comes to a stop."

"Ok!" Lorraina said in a nervous squeak.

"Ummm!" Krista said, in a panicked stutter. "Ummm!!!" Krista panicked again and again, louder and louder like a broken record. "Ummm, Lorraina!!!"

"What, Krista?" Richard blurted, looking over his shoulder and recognizing instantly what she was concerned about.

"Lorraina?... Let's practice slowing down like I just talked about a second ago" Richard said, as calmly as possible.

"I actually think I got the hang of this. I want to keep going. Can I turn onto the highway to take you to get your car now? Then I'll just follow you. It's getting dark now, and there won't be too many people out, so maybe I can just follow you."

Lorraina was finally feeling more sure of herself and wanted Richard to be proud of her. She wished he was her own dad or grandpa, but was really glad that she could do this and felt a great sense of accomplishment.

"Actually Lorraina, on second thought, I think I'm going to forget my car for now and drive you to my house myself. We'll figure out what to do, and then my wife can help me get the car, later" Richard said, in a bit of a panicked tone. "I think you should slow down now, and practice bringing the car to a stop, and we can switch." Richard became very adamant and a tinge snappy.

"Why?" Lorraina raised her voice. "Why can't either of you be proud of me? I'm doing good at this!" She hit the steering wheel with her hand. "I finally feel like there is something I'm good at and you want me to quit."

"It's not that at all Lorraina!" Richard insisted. "Please, this is not the time for this. Just stop the car and I will explain."

"No!" Lorraina shot back, rarely standing up for herself, or for what she wanted, at least towards authority figures. "I'm not stopping until you answer me. Why do I have to stop?"

"Because there is a snake in the car climbing up your seat and almost about to slither onto your neck and we really don't want to die." Richard said in an aggressive, frustrated voice.

"Oh brother." Lorraina said, rolling her eyes. "And I'm supposed to fall for that again" she said, as calm as mid-day. "You lied about the tarantula, you lied about the water pump, and both of those were to control me. Now you don't want to give me any credit for being a good driver and you want to take over and drive now, so you're lying to try to control me again." Lorraina chattered on as she continued driving at accelerated speeds, round and round the building.

"Krista?" she questioned. "Krista?" When there was no response from Krista, she asked "What's a matter with her?" to Richard.

"Well" he said, now leaning his body fearfully against the passenger seat window and door, and looking back toward Krista. "She passed out, I believe, from fright. Please slow down?" he pleaded.

Looking into the rear view mirror to check on Krista, to see why she wasn't responding. Lorraina could barely see in the ever dimming light. Krista was unconscious. Next to Lorraina, a slithering visitor was beginning to slime onto her shoulder. Black and white triangular patterns adorned its' body in strong contrast.

Lorraina took her foot instantly off of the gas, but hadn't been experienced in driving long enough to remember Richard's advice to gradually push the brake-pedal. As the four-foot long creeper slithered against her neck, Lorraina couldn't help it. Her foot slammed on the brake.

Skidding, with the left, tail-end of the car spinning out, and beginning to lose control, the vehicle collided with one of the two-and-a-half-foot boulders lined in a row of them, used as markers to mark the edge of the dusty driveway. This sent Mr. Avera's car further out of control, contacting another boulder, and scraping up the side. It slid on the powdery half-dirt, half-gravel road until it came to a complete stop.

CHAPTER 23

"Bridget!" Liam shouted from a small area upstairs in the apartment behind Bridget's boardwalk shop. "Bridget!" he hollered again, with a slight sound of panic and concern that was clearly audible now.

"What's the matter?" she answered, out of breath after she ran up the timeworn, steep, attic-stairs. The stairs led up to two extremely small rooms. They could never legally be called bedrooms due to their short height, lack of closets, small windows in the dormers, etc. "What happened, Liam? How did you even know this was up here? I blocked it off."

"I used to live here with my family. Of course, I know that it's here. I snuck up here and slipped past the shelf you placed in front of the steps, as soon as you left for the bathroom. It's so different in here. Why did you have to ruin it?"

"Ruin it? It looks exactly like it did when I bought the place. I just never did anything with it yet. I wasn't sure what I wanted to do with the space for sure. I have a few ideas, but it's so small" she said, feeling around till she found the battery-powered lantern that she'd left upstairs. Flicking it on, she could see cobwebs and dust and the lovely vintage wall papers. "Maybe someday I'll save myself money and move in instead of renting. Maybe you can live in one side and I'll take the other"

Bridget said, laughing. "I'm just kidding, it's just too small" Bridget said, shutting off the lantern and turning her back towards the area.

"Of course it's too small when you chop the rooms in half and lower the ceilings" Liam said, flipping the light back on. "This is not how the attic really looks. It was big once."

"Honey, everything looks bigger in your memories. Then you grow up and everything appears smaller. Nothing shrank, you just got bigger. That's life for everyone."

"But Bridget, I'm serious. This is not just memories. This is reality. This was not the original wall paper or ceiling. I didn't forget. This is not where or how the wall ended." He said, snatching the lantern out of her hand, and running up to the wall, dropping to his knees, and feeling the wallpaper with his free hand. Setting the lantern on the floor in front of his knees, he used both hands and began to work his fingers under the wall paper and the wall.

BOOM! BOOM! BOOM! BOOM!

Loud thudding knocks were heard below on the shop's front door. Both of them stiffened and tensed, eyes widening intensely and rapidly. "Who in the world could that be this time of evening?" Bridget whispered fearfully, with her voice cracking.

"I don't know! I hope it's not my dad!" Liam said, equally afraid.

"Did you tell him you were coming here?"

"No!"

"Then it's not going to be your dad!" Bridget whisper/yelled. "Should we just ignore it, and hide, or should we go see who it is?" Bridget questioned herself out loud, barely audible over the sound of the now fully raging storm.

"They can see your car outside, whoever it is, and they probably already know we're here or they wouldn't be out knocking on the door in this weather." Liam was intelligent beyond many children his age.

"Yah, but what if it's Utopia coming for you?" Bridget blurted, just above a whisper.

"They won't know I'm here, if you don't tell them." Liam responded, calmly. "Besides, what if it's your family who is worried that you never showed up?" Liam asked.

"They never could have gotten here by now." Bridget responded, as she reached the bottom of the steps. "But I have to be brave. I'm not going to open it, unless I'm safe..." she said. "But you had better stay in here and wait, in case it is Utopia." She added, sliding the bookshelf in front of the stairwell with Liam behind it.

As Bridget snuck through the house quietly, she was very grateful that she was so clean and orderly, as it made sneaking in the dark much easier. Large flood lights were flashing into the shop now and as Bridget barely opened the floor-length curtain between the apartment and shop. She was seen through the window, and she saw them. The blue and red strobing lights, on the top of the local law enforcement vehicle, were actually quite a relieving sight, to Bridget.

Flooding emotions came over her. Mostly comfort that the police must be there to check on her safety, and maybe to discuss her earlier encounter with Hayden. She considered it, and then realized that it was not the normal hour, or weather conditions, for such a visit. She knew she'd been seen through the window and decided to find out what they were there for.

"Hello, Miss," the younger, more energetic officer began, "Are you alright?" Giving her no time to answer, he continued on. "This is Sergeant McLellan and I'm Officer Fernandez." He stated formally, then stepped back and motioned slightly to his superior.

"We are here to inform you that you are in danger. This storm has picked up and intensified. We are not sure if you have any internet or have been paying attention to your phone, but we've put out an evacuation alert to everyone's phones and it's all over the news." The much-older Sergeant McLellan proceeded.

"I lost my phone in the slats of the boardwalk outside, and I have no access to internet or phone or anything. I didn't know. I was planning to camp out here till the storm passed."

"That is not a safe option, Miss, there is a very real threat of a tsunami and we are on full alert for this whole coastline. All the way from here to Alaska, one direction and all the way across the coast of Oregon and even California in the other direction."

"Ma'am, this is a mandatory evacuation!" Officer Fernandez repeated urgently. "We don't have time for chit chat. Most of the power is out in the area, I'm very shocked you still have any, which is actually the only reason that we even realized that anyone was here, the lights you know? And then we saw your car, figured you needed help, or that you were some old lady who didn't have any internet or phone."

"Well, I'm not old, but you are right, I don't have internet or my phone, as I mentioned – which is why I am scared to go anywhere with no phone, in this weather."

"What is your name, Ma'am?" asked the senior officer, with silver and white-infused, reddish hair, obviously attempting to look out for her welfare. "What can we do to help you get out of here?"

"Bridget Buchannon!" she told the friendly, plain-looking sergeant with the typical cliché "copstache". "My name is Bridget Buchannon" she repeated, a little fearful as she tried to take in all of the information.

"Does your vehicle work?" he was quickly attempting to find ways to do his duty and get her to safety and move on, to any others who may still be out in the storm.

"Yes, I believe so. It worked this morning, last time I used it."

"Ma'am, please gather your most valuable, irreplaceable items, and we will escort you to your vehicle to ensure that it works. We'll give you two minutes. That's all we have."

"My nephew is inside, resting." She responded. "It's going to take a bit longer than that."

"Ten minutes maximum, Miss Buchannon!" Officer McLellan said, obviously perturbed by the situation.

"Show us which board on the board-walk your phone is under, and we'll try to get it out, while we wait." Officer Fernandez piped up. "I wouldn't want my wife and nephew out on a night like this, especially with no phone or way to get help. I know your phone is going to have to dry out for quite some time, if it will ever work again from this weather, but I'm just trying to help."

Bridget pointed out from the doorway to the board on the walk, with the large knot, and a slight gap between the two boards. "That was the one that it had fallen through," Bridget declared.

"We'll get right to it, and then you can borrow my phone to call your family, and let them know where you are. I'm sure they're worried sick." Officer Fernandez concluded, walking over to the boardwalk, as Bridget quickly went inside and shut the door.

Immediately she rushed to the steps and moved the bookshelf. "It was the policemen, Liam" she informed him. "There is a huge storm and they need to escort us out of here and make sure we leave safely. We have no time! We have to go now! None of my super important stuff is here, at this house, so I guess I don't have time to do anything but update you."

"For now, I told the police that you are my nephew, and that is all they need to hear. I will do the talking to them, if anything needs to be said about that. I'm not concerned about these policemen, they seem very nice. It's Utopia's guards that we have to really look out for. I don't want these guys turning you over to them. They are just trying to help get my cell phone out from underneath the boardwalk." Bridget was interrupted by another tap at the door.

"Ok, they're ready for us" she said, leaving him at the entrance to the apartment, looking into the shop, and rushing across to get the door.

"Grab your jacket" she said, looking at him over her shoulder as she grabbed the door handle. "Even if it's wet, we can dry it later; just don't put it on yet" she concluded, turning back to let the policemen know they were almost ready.

Gasping, Bridget fell back a step. When she had turned her face back around toward the door. Instead of the police officers that she was expecting, it was almost as if she were staring in a mirror... only a mirror that aged her by twenty years.

"Tyrnia!?" Bridget's mouth gaped and her breath was nearly taken. She said this, as she recalled her run-in with Hayden, earlier that day, when he mistook her for someone he had called Tyrnia.

"Mom!" Liam shouted, running full force to hug his mom.

"Don't Liam! Stop son. Please!" she pled.

He froze in his tracks, just as he approached her. "Why? Why don't you want me?"

"Oh Liam," her eyes pierced into his soul as she crouched down near him. "It's not that. I have a sort of order – an order that says I'm not allowed to touch you – it's sort of like a restraining order. It is extremely complicated, and I really am not allowed to tell you the details."

She went on, tears streaming down her face, "I want to hold you and touch your hair and face and arm. I want to hug you! Don't you believe otherwise, not for one split second! But... I broke some serious rules. I went against important laws and I made an awful choice that landed me where I'm at."

Liam was confused, his eyebrows knit together in anger and he wanted to break something or hit someone. He wanted to fight whomever was making this law, and keeping him from her. He visibly expressed his feelings in that regard, balling up his fist and swinging at an invisible opponent, then continued talking through his punches. "Why won't they let me hug you? That is just mean! I hate cops!" he yelled. "No wonder people hate cops! Why did they even bring you to me, if I'm not allowed to hug you?"

"They didn't even know you were here, Liam. I just hoped that you might be and wanted to drop something off. Don't be mad at them. They are trying to help you. They are just doing their job. If you're going to be mad, be upset at me. I'm the one who messed up Liam. It's my fault that I can't be with you all of the time anymore. I'm just so thankful that I'm given the chance to see you at all, even just for a few minutes. I've gotta keep the rules from now on, you know? So that someday we can be together. I'm willing to keep all the rules now, and sacrifice anything, and everything, so I can see you again, and hold you again, and live with you again! Do you hear me?"

"Yes, Mom I hear you! But it's so unfair! It's not my fault that you made bad choices, so why are they punishing me?"

"You're so right son! It's not your fault at all and not your responsibility at all, but it's something that is too complicated to explain right now, and I don't have time. Nobody means to punish you. There's just a lot of messed up stuff in the world right now and most people are just trying to do their job, and survive. They aren't punishing you. My choices did that, and for that,

I am so very sorry! I never realized that my bad choices would hurt you. I didn't think it through. I just thought... well, it really doesn't matter what I thought. I have to do my time now, to make things right, and I want to make it up to you, eventually somehow, so we can be together again."

"Mom, can I live with this nice lady then, if I can't live with you? Can you give the police permission? We told them that she is my aunt. Until you are better, please? I can't live with dad anymore! He is too mean and he won't stop drinking." Liam pleaded with his mother.

"Liam, Bridget is your aunt actually, so you have nothing to worry about. That is the truth. Stay with her and the paperwork that you need, to verify that, will turn up soon."

"Turn up?" Bridget questioned. She was a little frustrated and overwhelmed at what odd timing this was, and all of the pressure that this woman was putting on such a young man. Also, the surprise that Tyrnia claimed that she was somehow related to her, was a little much for her to handle, at the moment, and she was feeling very lied to. "Turn up?" she asked again.

"Well, yes, I will get it to you, I mean. You don't have time now, but most of what you will need I sealed in the walls upstairs. Everything is in water-tight containers and will be safe through the storm. Please just don't let Utopia take my son. They took our other five boys and it destroyed us. They may be my adopted sons, but that makes no difference to me, they also were my boys."

"I won't let them take him Ma'am."

"But Mom, why doesn't Bridget know you, if you are her sister? And what about Grandma and Grandpa Zaugg?"

"Honey, I'm out of time. Your questions will be answered; your quest to figure it all out without me has begun. It actually began a long time ago, since we last said goodbye. The policemen are going to be getting anxious and wondering why you are taking so long. They have other people to save."

"But why didn't you write me? Why didn't you call? When can I see you again? Can I..."

"I wrote you over a hundred letters Liam, they are hidden up in the wall along with your heirloom horse I passed on to you. And you know your father wouldn't have let me call!" Tyrnia continued.

"Does he know where you are, Mom? Have you even spoken to him?

"No, he knows nothing. Please tell him for me, later when you are up to it, if you can. I'm ordered not to speak to him at all. My time is up. I have to go! I left a special gift for you. The officers will bring it to you. It's a game. Nothing too special, just something I made to sell in this shop a long time ago. It was the prototype: the only one, but I never finished making it. It's all I had to leave you, aside from all the letters and papers and old photos, hidden in the wall." Tyrnia paused after she started toward the door, she turned back to look at Liam, "I have to go. I love you!"

Tyrnia fiercely brushed away her tears and turned sharply. She stopped completely at the door again, and said, with her back still toward them, "This is the hardest thing I have ever had to do, ever! Keeping the rules like this, not to touch and hold you Liam... I love you! I just can't..." and she exited through the door, abruptly closing it behind her.

CHAPTER 24

Another tap at the door and then, before Bridget could open it, Officer Fernandez opened the shop door. "We really have to leave this minute. We got another call to respond to; in addition to that, this storm is worsening! We're waiting for more details about where to go to help somebody, but the second we hear more, we have to go" he said, holding the door open for them to exit.

"We gave you as long as we possibly could. I don't have time for you to even borrow my phone now, but if you give me the name and number of who to call, I will try and call somebody for you, when I get a break. Here is your cell phone. It is completely drenched, so don't try and turn it on yet. I guess you probably already know that though. And here is a game that..."

"We need to go now!" Sergeant McLellan hollered from outside cutting him off. "We have to go! A tree fell on an elderly man. You need to call for backup Fernandez, for us to get that tree off of him." The sergeant commanded hurriedly. "Nice meeting you Ma'am. Please get out of here now! This is a big one" he said, shutting the car door abruptly.

"Sorry we couldn't be of more assistance, Miss" Officer Fernandez began to say, as the power flickered and then went off completely – leaving it dangerously dark outside. "We'll try to stop back by later, to make sure you got out ok" he concluded, rushing off.

Liam was still holding the battery-powered lantern and Bridget quickly turned on a flash light. She handed Liam the game, from his mother, locked the door, and they headed off to her car.

CHAPTER 25

"I guess we have to spend Christmas in the hospital, Mr. Baulmfield." Aleta said to her husband, as she twirled some strange noodle concoction on her plate in the hospital cafeteria. "If we're going to spend it with our son anyway" she finished, staring off at nothing.

"I am well aware that it would never be Christmas to you, honey, if we celebrated it without him" her husband said, reaching over and taking her hand, pulling her to him in a comforting manner. "He's done a lot of crazy things in his life and we've spent a lot of days, and holidays, with him in the hospital, but at least we have him still. He keeps us on our toes, keeps us young, and keeps life interesting for us."

"Yah" Mrs. Baulmfield responded, sitting up more and pulling away from their momentary embrace. "Remember the time that he put a popcorn kernel up his nose and we were in here for three or four hours before the PA finally came in and said, 'Ok , Mamma, you plug the opposite nostril and blow into his mouth.' Then it popped right out in one second." Donna laughed a little as she reminisced, "I was so mad. I'm still mad that they didn't just tell me what to do over the phone, when I called ahead. That would have saved so much time, and money, and headache. Remember?"

"For sure, how could I ever forget? It seems funny now that I look back on it, but man was I upset when I wasted so much time worried, panicked, with a fussy kid at the Emergency Room and with such a giant bill later. All I have to say is: thank goodness for insurance with this son of ours, or we would have been broke by now."

Mr. Baulmfield thought for a moment, his eyes off in the distance, with a bit of a knowing smile. He continued, "Like the time he swallowed that toy globe, that came with the doll house, and the time he swallowed a penny, and the time he got his fingertip chopped off in the solid oak doorway at the church, and when the ambulance came that time that his seizure lasted for an hour, but I couldn't get back from work soon enough, and you were so mad at me. Man, the list could go on and on forever."

"It sure could... but he has been a really good son overall. I mean, at least all of those things that he went to the hospital for were not his fault. He never did anything harmful to anyone else, at least, and he never intentionally hurt us or got himself hurt" Aleta said in a defensive tone.

"Give me a break Aleta! Are you forgetting everything? Those things we just reminisced about might not have been his fault, just a curious kid, but if you are honest with yourself, you know that he has caused a lot of his own heart aches and others'. What about the time he tied his friend Jerry up to a trash can after dressing him up in snow clothes and then lighting fireworks off under him?"

"Well that was one time, and he was only 9 years old!"

"I guess you expect me to believe he was being nice, because he dressed him in snow clothes, so that it wouldn't hurt Jerry as much? Aleta, I know that you love him, I do too, but he's been a little harder to raise than you seem to allow yourself to remember sometimes."

"I know Ben, but I'm just so worried about him, especially right now. I am trying to think of all of the good things and forget the bad. I know that they asked us to help go over all of his history, fill out all of this paperwork, and assist with his psychological profile, but all I can focus on right now is the possibility that Hayden's birth mother is right in this very hospital. That she might meet our son, whom she gave away, and didn't want, and he might want to call her mom, and not me."

"Oh honey, don't be ridiculous! I know you are emotional and worried, but he's not just going to forget us. And I don't think that she..."

"I don't know how I feel about that woman right now, Ben! Don't call me emotional and ridiculous! You know that I even used to be grateful to her, that she gave him his life, and all. But now, right now, I feel angry that her genetics may have given him this health concern or whatever is wrong with him. What if I have to meet her? What if she's rude to me or him? What if..."

"Honey, just stop doing this to yourself. You can only solve the world's problems one at a time, and that was way more than one problem you just mentioned." Ben said, jokingly to his wife.

Interrupting their conversation came an uneasy voice, "Excuse me, are you guys here for a son that is acting strangely?" Mr. Hessop asked in an uneven, emotional tone. It was obvious that he'd been crying, and was very much out of his comfort zone. "I couldn't help but overhear part of your conversation, and my wife has been in here for hallucinating, and acting very crazy and out of sorts. We have been told that they are checking her DNA for a match with, I presume, your son."

"Yes! We are here for him." Ben Baulmfield answered, as his wife looked at the floor to avoid tears.

"Well, I don't know exactly what to say" James Hessop responded, "But I do want you to know, that my wife is a very good woman. I really can't say that I know why she adopted him out, or if he's even her son, as we've been married many, many years and she's never breathed a word of it to me." James choked on his words a little and swallowed hard and then continued.

"But I can say that if he is hers, if she had a son, she would have had to have a serious reason to let him go. She is a very good woman and very mother-like, even though we were never able to have any of our own. She would never try to steal him from you. If he is hers, I imagine she would almost worship you and grovel at your feet, wanting to thank you so much for raising him, when she couldn't."

Without any pause or giving Mr. or Mrs. Baulmfield a chance to respond or interject at all, Mr. Hessop chattered on. "I just want you to know that while I had nothing to do with it, I feel personally sorry to you for the pain you're experiencing here, and I can relate to the shock factor a little. I hope you are still able to have a nice Christmas together, at least, and at least you have each other and your son" James Hessop said, with a broken heart. He stood there at their table briefly and then turned to walk off.

"Mister???" Ben questioned. "We don't even know your name!"

"Mr. Hessop, or James is fine. Sorry, I forgot to tell you, and yours?" he said, holding back his emotions.

"Ben, and my wife here is Aleta. Sorry you are going through such a 'nice patch' of life too" Ben said, sarcastically. "We appreciate you approaching us and trying to reach out. It's just a lot for my wife to take in. She just needs some space, please... but thank you for trying to help."

"Actually, it's ok." Aleta cut in. "I never thought of it from someone else's point of view, their struggle and pain before. It makes it a little easier to bear."

"Mrs. and Mr. Baulmfield, can I speak with you a moment, please?" Hayden's replacement nurse began.

"Whatever you have to say, our friend can hear too." Mr. Baulmfield expressed, standing and patting Mr. Hessop's shoulder.

"Your choice, I guess." The nurse said. "For now, the only response from the doctor is that he's busy working on your cases. Oh yeah, and also that the maternity test was inconclusive or altered somehow. The doctor is looking into it, but will be available for emergencies only, during Christmas break. So, we are not going to have any answers over the next couple of days. Sorry for the inconvenience" he concluded.

CHAPTER 26

Pulling into the driveway of his small stucco, suburban home in Mesa, Arizona, Richard was both relieved and petrified to be there and see his wife. Thankful that the vehicle of Mr. Avera's, not only was still drivable, but that they managed to get that far with nobody noticing that they were in Mr. Avera's car.

The back drivers-side of the car was crumpled, and after such an intense day it was a wonder that all three of them were not asleep upon their arrival, versus just Lorraina and Krista sleeping. They were asleep in the back next to each other, as they were both too afraid to be alone after their run-in with the California kingsnake.

Thankfully, this snake was not deadly, not even venomous. Due to the intensity and suddenness of the swerving and hitting the rocks, the snake did not bite and was flung off of Lorraina. It had landed at Richard's feet. He had quickly exited the car and left the door open and sort of shooed it out of the car with a stick that he found lying outside, near the car.

"Finally, I'm home!" Richard proclaimed loudly, to wake up Krista and Lorraina. "Would you guys wake up, please? I have a lot of explaining to do about all of this to my wife. She doesn't know the half of what I do at work, because I felt it better than making her worry all the time. I didn't want her to tell me that she's worried about me working for Mr. Avera."

"Wait a minute!" Lorraina started, wide awake now. "So, your wife doesn't even know where you work?" she asked, knitting her eyebrows together in an irritated scowl. "So, you think your little 'white' lies can keep someone from being disappointed in you? Or keep them from their choice of response or interaction? You lie, so that you can be in control, as I said earlier. I have witnessed this type of behavior many times from people in my life. Like I said, Richard Perecha, 'the end never justifies the means.' Never!"

"It's so not cool that you feel it's ok to lie to your wife and do whatever you want to do for work, and then justify it and ask for forgiveness afterwards, after you got to do what you wanted." Lorraina said, shutting the car door and straightening out her jump suit.

Lorraina was very irritated by finding out that Richard was keeping such a big secret from his wife, especially after he had lied to her a couple of times. "That stupid saying 'it's better to ask for forgiveness than permission' is some crazy excuse to justify dishonesty. If there's anything in this world that I hate, it's dishonesty. Tell me something that I don't want to hear, but if it's the truth – at least I have the choice about how to respond. I don't have to like it, want it, be ok with it, or agree with it, but at least I can make my choice of how I react or choose to react to it, if it's honest and sincere. I despise lies and I assume your wife does too. Most people do, and if she's anything like I imagined her, and if she is a good woman, like you said she is, than she's going to be very..."

"Ok!" Richard barked. "That's enough, you know-it-all! My wife's already going to yap my ear off and probably send me out to sleep in the barn with the chickens; I don't need you two to lecture my ears off." He snapped at them, notably concerned about his wife's reaction as he walked up the three steps and unlocked the door that went into the house from the garage.

"I didn't even say anything, Richard" Krista defended herself.

"And you won't" he ordered, as he finally got the door unlocked. "I will do all of the talking" he said, flinging the door open.

"Honey... I'm home! Victoria, I brought company!" He gave a warning that was heard throughout the freezing, dark house. Richard could hear a faint home video playing on the television. He had that one very memorized; his wife had watched it so often since their grandchildren were taken. This time it was quieter than usual and there were no lights on, which was also unusual for his wife.

It was late, but only about 1:00 am. Richard and the girls had been staying on back roads as much as possible. To their advantage, they passed a bunch of odd cars who were towing other cars with piles of stuff on top of both the car pulling and the car being towed. That drew way more attention to those vehicles, and away from Mr. Avera's car that the three of them were escaping in. Two of the six of these strange caravans of cars were pulled over by the local authorities and Richard was able to get home without being stopped.

"Victoria?! Are you home?" Richard called. "Baby it's freezing in here!" he hollered, walking over to the thermostat for the air conditioning. After setting the temperature from 62° to 72°, he shut off the television. There was still no sign of her, so he checked their bedroom.

"Victoria?!?" he shouted, thinking maybe she got carried away reading, scrapbooking, or sewing, off somewhere in the house. He didn't see her in the bedroom, which was still clean, bed made, and everything normal.

"Maybe she left your lying butt!" Krista blurted out. "She doesn't like you telling her that you'll do the talking" she laughed a little, and infused heavy sass into her tone.

"You know, this is not a good time!" Richard darted a glare at her and then glanced over with the same type of warning sign to Lorraina.

The regular house lights were all off. Holly interspersed with white lights – twisted around the evergreen garland, which was wrapped around the stair railing and the balustrade, which was overlooking the living area – gave off enough light for them to get around. In addition to the glimmering from the garland-lights, an ornate, medieval-themed, Christmas tree illuminated the room. One could see most things needed to be seen without the lights on.

Richard was nervous. It was not typical for his wife to be away from home. She was always in bed by 1:00 am, unless he was late from work, and then she was habitually watching family re-runs on the couch, not gone anywhere. He began racing around the house, turning all the lights on, as he called for her.

Lorraina and Krista looked at each other fearfully. Insecurity and confusion replaced their sass and confidence, as they both recognized that Richard hadn't shown any fear till now. They had been hoping that Mrs. Perecha would be a kind, warm, motherly person who would comfort them, be a role model, and maternal mentor. They wished for comfort now, more than before, seeing that the only safe adult that either of them had been around in a long while, was in utter panic.

"Richard!" Krista called out to him. "I see somebody!" She had no clue what she was looking for, but she saw some movement, either someone or something. "Richard, there's a leg sticking out from behind your Christmas tree!" she shouted more frantically. "It moved!" She squeaked, in fear.

"Is it Victoria?" he asked, running up from the basement, winded now completely.

"How should I know? I neva seen her and I only sees a leg. Ahhhhhh!!!" Krista screeched, "I'm too scared! Do ya' think I'm gonna go check a body dat might be a robber? It might be dead or dying? Heck, no! Heck no!" Krista repeated herself, in conclusion.

Richard ran behind the nine-foot Christmas tree, completely ornate with spectacular ornaments and unique one-of-a-kind treasures.

"Victoria!? What happened?" he asked her, "Are you alright?"

"I was trying to place ornaments on the back of the tree." She spoke almost in a whisper. "I can't move. I'm in pain and I need help." Her words were broken, slurred and weak.

"You're burning up and freezing at once, babe!" he proclaimed, after checking her forehead and face and feeling her cold arms and body against him.

"Help me up please?" she asked quietly. "I need my peppermint oil." Victoria coughed and held her chest. Then she coughed vigorously, dry like a seal. Richard grabbed her peppermint oil from her vest pocket, that she hadn't been able to get to, and placed a couple drops straight onto her tongue. Victoria used it often, to relax the tightness in her lungs, opened her airways, and to help relieve her gastric coughing.

"Can you guys give me a hand?" Richard knew that he could not lift her by himself, as he was in too much pain from arthritis and walking so far earlier that day. They had all been through a lot, so he motioned to them in desperation. Krista and Lorraina came over and helped us much as they could to get Victoria over to the couch. "Grab blankets," he ordered them, in an authoritative manner. He was not thinking of manners or asking please, as he was in fear for his wife.

"Where from?" Krista yelled as she ran around in a panic, not knowing what to do or where to get the blankets.

"In that small closet right straight to the left." Richard responded, as he held Victoria's hand. "Have you had any medicine?" he asked his wife. "Anything to take down the swelling, or to get this fever down?"

"No, not at all yet." Victoria Perecha weakly mumbled, as Krista brought some blankets from the linen cupboard. "I didn't realize that I had a fever".

"Go get some liquid fever and pain reducer from the left-hand top shelf in the door of my fridge, would you?" Richard gave his directions to Krista. She didn't normally like to be directed or told what to do, but she was very concerned about Mrs. Perecha. So, she quickly and quietly did as she was asked. Richard could see from Lorraina and Krista's faces, they were curious.

"It says 'Children's'" Krista said.

"I know she's not a little kid, but she doesn't swallow or absorb pills very well, so liquid works better and faster for proper absorption, and so that she can get it down. She really has a strong gag reflex, and chokes when she tries to swallow most medication" he said.

"You knew your health wouldn't allow you to get up there!" he snapped at his wife. In his mind it was out of concern, but he was not showing it very well to her or others. Whenever he was afraid or concerned, he got more gruff and demanding. "Stop scaring me like this, babe! You know your legs fall out from under you, so why would you choose to do something like that while I'm gone?!" he continued, barely taking a pause as he nearly yelled at her, fearfully.

"Gosh, stop yellin' at her Bro!" Krista butted in. "Here ya were afraid she wuz gonna yell at you for lying, and yur the one who is yellin' 'nd being rude."

"I'm not yelling! I'm just expressing how worried I am. My wife knows me, that's how I show my concern and protect her." Richard defended his behavior.

"Wow! Ya had me fooled!" Krista scoffed.

"So glad I ain't stuck as yur wife!" Krista said, rolling her eyes and finishing padding the blanket up and around Mrs. Perecha.

"I have to agree with Krista on this one Richard! You know how I feel about lying. I guess I can also tell you how much I can't stand too much pride and an ego that is over the top. You can't just yell at your wife, tell her what to do, and then say that it is because you love her, and it is your way of showing you care."

Richard glared at both of them, trying to hold back a response. "Grrrr, whatever! I can show my love in whatever way that I want to, especially in my own house, and you two should feel thankful and lucky that I saved your butts. Stay out of my relationship!"

There had been no verbal response yet from Victoria. She only smirked at their comments and laughed a little when the girls were sharing their observations and opinions with Richard. Then after Richard's response, she closed her eyes and gloomily leaned back a little. Tired and exhausted, sick, Victoria dreaded hearing the next "story" of how these two women ended up in her house in the middle of the night, when Richard hadn't responded to her phone calls or messages all day. She waited in a moment of silence.

"I know, I'm sorry... I know you're probably thinking I'm crazy and you're totally confused and another hairbrained scheme of mine is going to ruin another holiday, but it just isn't like that, Victoria. It really wasn't my fault this time, and it just sort of all happened. I couldn't let them die! I couldn't just ignore them, when they needed help."

She rolled her eyes behind her closed eye lids and turned her face away. "Come on honey, you rejecting me and being sad and disappointed in me is worse than if you were just yelling, cuz I can just out-yell you. But you know that, so of course you're going to ignore me."

"Richard," she began, slowly and with frailty. "You know I have had enough pain and trauma to last three people's life times." There was a slight pause and a deep sigh... "Don't cause any more!" she said intently, defining her boundary, but not in a cruel or mean voice. Exhaustion and depletion had overtaken her, and sleep was nearly all that she could dwell on, but she pushed herself through.

"I have no idea what is going on, and no one wants to begin to imagine all of the horrors that my vivid imagination have conjured up today, so I am trying to just ignore and recoup" she responded partially, and rested her head again. "It's Christmas Eve already." She whispered, "Please don't ruin it, don't yell, don't taint one more memory."

"Mrs. Perecha," Lorraina began. "I can tell how tired you are, and how sick, but it's really not as bad as you think. A lot of it is not his fault actually. You see, he got kicked out of his job at Utopia for helping me, and then they told him he 'gets' to kill me. I was scared, so I ran after him with my luggage and he kept walking away. We got all the way to his other job, at the sewage place, and then the bad guys came. Oh yeah, and he lied to me about a tarantula, which I was pretty mad about, but that was to save me from Mr. Avera's guards, who were talking about framing Mr. Avera, and having data on him. Then they said Richard could hurt as many girls as he wants to for all they care. So, they aren't worried about finding him, because they thought he was in the middle of killing me."

Victoria's eyes were open, shocked, and she was listening intently, but still very weak.

"Then they said they were going to kill Krista. Then we went to a surveillance room and watched them as they threw her in the sewage pit. Then, when they drove away, we ran down to save her. I couldn't do much to help, but I was brave enough to deal with the smell. But Richard dove into the poop swamp and got Krista and then we all had to get cleaned up. That's why we're wearing these ugly Utopia jumpsuits. Then we took Mr. Avera's car and Richard tried to teach us how to drive. Then Krista got out of the car and it was my turn, and then while I was driving there, there was this freaky snake with black and white triangles on it, and then I crashed and Richard got the snake away. Then he drove here, while Krista and I slept in the back seat, and then we found you on the floor behind the Christmas tree." Lorraina finally stopped for a long breath.

"Oh," Krista said, "That's what happened before you got me out."

"Well not everything, I didn't tell you about the day before, the first day that I left."

"That's enough!" Richard interrupted. "Do you have any idea how crazy that sounds, when you just said it like that? You just made it worse and made me sound like a freaking lunatic!"

"Yeah, I guess it does sound pretty bad."

"I'm super thankful that Richard saved me though, Ma'am." Krista said, looking for a response from Victoria.

"I can see that you are hoping for a response from me, right now" Victoria said, with a blank and sickly look on her face. "But I honestly have no idea how to respond right now, or what to say, except that at least finally that would explain your awful smell."

She breathed through the blanket for a second to avoid the smell. "I'm not sure of your name, young lady," she said, turning a little toward Lorraina, "But that is actually much worse than I thought. And you mean to tell me, that Mr. Avera's car is damaged, and it's in our garage?!" her voice was finally elevated in spite of her illness.

Victoria frantically sat up straight. "I hope this is a nightmare!" Victoria buried her face in her hands, pulling at the roots of her hair, trying to ignore what she had heard and wishing she could just un-hear it.

"Well, I am Lorraina, and this is Krista and we are here to help you in any way we can, since your husband saved us and he says you are a good woman."

Victoria looked up parting her hands and glaring at Richard through her fingers. "We are definitely going to have to have a serious talk later! I can't even think right now. I am so tired and my head is pounding from this headache or fever or whatever." Victoria scowled up at Richard.

"Do you need me to take you to the hospital?" Richard asked his wife.

"In Mr. Avera's crashed car?" she questioned.

"Victoria, I'm sorry. I can fill in the blanks later. I'll explain."

"Yeah, like you always do, excusing your lies. I'm very glad that you saved these two young women, but lying to me about where you work is not re-building trust from the last hundred lies. No matter how you try and justify it, it's never ok to lie to me. I'm too exhausted and sick to even discuss anything further. I've lived with it this long, I will have to deal with it another night."

"I have to go get rid of Mr. Avera's car while it's still night." Richard said somberly, knowing how much he'd hurt and disappointed his wife again. "I'll be back as soon as I can." He turned towards the garage after putting on some new rubber gloves to keep his finger prints off of the vehicle.

"Richard..." Victoria said in a pleading tone. "Please, I still love you. I just can't be happy about lies, and I'm very concerned about your safety right now and..." she shook her head, trying to figure out what to even say. "Please be safe and careful. I do want to see you again even if I'm upset at you. And I don't understand why you have to get rid of Mr. Avera's car tonight, what is going on here? Did you actually kill somebody?"

"No! Of course not!" Richard exclaimed emphatically. He turned and walked across the room and stood above her. "I just don't have time to explain right now. You're going to have to trust me on this one" he said, about to walk away.

"Trust you? I don't even know you anymore... or the truth obviously. It's hard to believe that there is a real wolf, when the shepherd boy has cried 'wolf' one too many times. You know what I'm talking about."

Richard arrogantly looked down at her, with irritation toward her. He felt that he knew he was making the right plan for that moment, and she didn't – but also he felt intense irritation toward himself, recognizing that his past decisions, and his choice to not even tell her where he worked, were the reason she could not trust him.

His countenance mellowed, and he humbled himself a little, as he thought about what a mess he'd gotten her, and all of them, into – through his decisions, not hers at all. Here she had believed his lies again, worried about him all afternoon and evening, was sick with a fever, and now would be stuck caring for these two strangers, while he left her to try to fix things, once again. Richard felt sorry that something bad could happen to him, and she could be stuck fixing a problem she didn't understand, or possibly take the blame for something he drug her into, yet again.

"Call 911 if you get worse, and tell them I'm at work if they ask. I am anyway, that is the truth, just a different type of work. Make sure that Lorraina and Krista hide when they come, if they come. The people I work for are ruthless scoundrels, Victoria. I'm sorry that I never told you! Do not trust them. I know that you can't trust me, on everything right now, but you know that I would never murder anybody – at least you should know that!"

Richard looked off in the distance, at nothing in particular, and bit his lower lip a little in frustration, trying to let his own emotions cool off. In all somberness he looked back at his wife, "They would murder, Victoria... they have murdered, and they tried to today. They are going to be after us soon, if they are not already. Mr. Avera's guards believe the girls are both dead, but... I'm sorry that I got us into this mess, but this is all I have time for! I love you too! I'll be back as soon as I can" he concluded, leaning down and looking into Victoria's eyes.

He pulled her chin up, with his gloved hand. "I love you!" he said, with a fierce loyalty. "And one day, I'll make it up to you, and I'll make you truly proud... with no lies." Then he kissed her, and she kissed back, a tear now streaming down her cheek.

CHAPTER 27

"How long do ya think it's bin since he's bin gone?" Krista said, during a lull in the conversation.

"Who knows" Lorraina said. "I know it's been a long time though, because I slept in till noon, and we've been talking since then. I'm so glad you are feeling better today." Lorraina said, directed at Victoria Perecha.

"Thank you" Victoria responded. "I am feeling a lot better. I had been stuck laying on the floor for hours before you guys found me. I have a weird genetic arthritis and some crazy nerve damage and endocrine issues, that I'm sure you don't care for me to bore you with, but it means that I never really feel top notch. However, I am considerably better today than I was last night. Thank goodness for sleep!" She said, looking out the window, attempting to see Richard, and searching nervously off in the distance.

"I sure hope he comes home soon." Victoria began pacing the house and getting some dishes out.

"What are you going to make?" Lorraina asked her.

"Mince meat pies, cinnamon rolls, fruit cake, and just prep for the typical Christmas dinner I always make."

"Like what da heck else are you preppin' for?" Krista asked. "I ain't ever had that yummy of food since we bin at Utopia... or ever, for dat matter. What more could ya ax for?"

"Well..." Mrs. Perecha smiled and put her long, curly, dark hair up with a hair claw. "There will be turkey, mashed potatoes, gravy, deviled eggs, stuffing, rolls, cranberry sauce, yams, olives, pickles, sparkling cider, and I already made a blueberry pie, strawberry-rhubarb pie, banana cream and lemon meringue pies."

"Oh, my gosh! I think I've died and gone to heaven now. I don't remember anything even close to this good, or homemade, since I was at my grandma's house when I was 9. Actually, even that was nothing like this!" Lorraina, said enthusiastically.

"I wish I had ever gotten to experience anything at all like this. I've never had food like that, or that much of it anyway. I've only seen it in movies. I so wish!"

"Well, you get to, today, young ladies, and tomorrow. That is how we do Christmas around here. My kids and grandkids should be here around 6pm."

"Do you think Richard will be back by then?" Lorraina questioned.

"Who knows, but thankfully we have 4 hours till then. If we haven't seen him by the time our kids get here, then I guess we'll go find him."

"Sounds good, I guess." Krista said, looking somber and depressed.

Victoria noticed this and wanted to try to get her out of the gloom that had just taken up residence over her disposition. "So do you have any memories with any of your grandparents during Christmas time, Krista?" she asked, beginning to pour some flour into a large mixing bowl.

"I only have one memory with my grandma!" She said, looking at the floor and tapping her foot awkwardly.

"Is it a good one?" Victoria questioned, as she began mixing Christmas spices such as nutmeg, ginger, cinnamon, and cloves into the flour.

"I remember her face mostly. I was seven. I remember dat she had da tiniest little Christmas tree I ever seen.

It was glistnin' with tiny ornments 'nd little lights. The whole tree was five or maybe seven inches. I touched the tiny ornments. They were so detailed and wonderful." Krista paused, off in her memories for a moment.

"I asked my grandma where she got the tiny ornments from. Then she hand me two more 'n said, 'I got this one from your granddad the day we wuz tyin' da knot.'"

"Then she said I could hang the tiny little snowflake thing on the tree. She then tol' me dat the other one, she had gotten from gramps too, on a trip to New York. I put 'em on and then she finely ax me if I knew where she got 'em from. I had no idea what she was meanin' and she laughed, seein' me so confused.

She finely say, 'Honey girl, your granddad and I have never had money enough for things like Christmas trees. So one year, my daughter, yo' mama, went to dis tiny store in the mall with goodies fo' Christmas an' gots me dis here tree. I thought long and hard about how dat tree needed to be decorated, an' jus how I could maybe make tiny ornments outa foil or sompin', but I wanted to make sure dey wuz beautiful! So, I set dat tree on my shelf and went 'bout my day. Later on, I went to put on some earrin's and realize dat I wuz missin' the match to most every earrin' I had.'"

Krista smiled and played around with a fancy napkin on the table as she shared her distinctive memory of her grandmother. "She say, 'I came outa da room and axed yo' gramps if he knew what happened to my earrin's and he walked me ova there and lifted a handkerchief up off dat lil tree. It was all lit up purdy wit tiny LED lights, an' one of each of my earrin's... He died tree weeks later, and I ain't never gonna forget that special moment. I know you neva got ta meet him, but he woulda loved you so! And I bin decorating dat lil tree ever since, EVERY Christmas!'"

There was a pause and then sniffling; Krista used the back of her hand to wipe her face. "My grams died a few months after dat memry and joined my granddad. I think she missed him too much. I was purdy much on the streets after dat."

"Well," Victoria said touching Krista's shoulder. "That sounds like a pretty perfect last memory to me. I can tell your life has been tough since then, but we're going to just have to fix that, and make some awesome new memories this Christmas, ok?"

She paused for a second, "I do understand about tainted memories. However, I'd like to make some un-tainted ones the rest of this afternoon and evening, so I will teach you guys some new recipes." She then asked Lorraina and Krista to get various ingredients for her and began teaching them how to cook.

Police sirens began to be heard, increasingly becoming louder and ongoing. They grew ever-nearer, until they were deafening. Ambulance alerts were simultaneously fast approaching, as was a fire engine with its air horn. Just then, they heard a loud knock, thumping at the door, and hearts jumped into the throats of all three women.

"Get into the bedroom and hide!" Mrs. Perecha demanded, quietly. Lorraina and Krista readily obeyed, and she walked steadily to the front door, in an attempt to collect herself and appear unruffled.

CHAPTER 28

"Almost there" Bridget patted Liam's knee to wake him up. "Hey bud, we're going to be there at my mom's in a couple of turns."

"How many minutes is that?" Liam asked stretching and yawning.

"Not minutes" she said turning the third corner since her statement. "This is the last turn." Bridget said pulling up to a white iron gate with a security box and key pad. The gate connected to a white-coated iron fencing that laced the entire 18 acre parcel, making it very secure, but also exquisite. The grass was perfectly manicured, cut short like a golf course. There were lovely varieties of trees, flowers, and shrubbery all trimmed and trimmed to perfection.

"Wow! What the heck! Where are we?" Liam said, sitting upright, eyes widening as they pulled in through the gates, after Bridget had typed in the pass code and the gate rolled open. "This is astonishing Bridge. I can't even begin to believe that my eyes are actually seeing this. I thought that houses like this were only in movies. Your mom lives here?" Liam elevated his tone.

"Yes she does, but..."

"You never told me your mom was rich!"

"Whether she is or not... that shouldn't matter. However, I never told you that your grandma is rich, because she isn't."

"I don't understand." Liam hesitated.

"Well, she does live in this gorgeous, gated property, but not in the main house." Bridget said, driving past it. "She lives in the beautiful servant's quarters, or caretaker home. My mom is a maid." Bridget said with a confident smile.

"A maid? What's a maid?" Liam asked, inquisitively.

"A maid is a person who cleans up after others, and gets paid. Someone who orders things, changes light bulbs, washes dishes, straightens, you know, does everything the boss asks, for pretty much."

"Oh, you mean like a mom?" he asked innocently.

"Well, yeah, pretty much like a mom, only to take care of other moody, rude adults. But at least she gets paid." Bridget laughed a little.

"My mom is going to be so worried, and I have a lot of questions for her, and I want us to open that game that your mom made and gave to you. Plus, I wonder..."

A rap-tapping was lightly struck on the driver's side window of Bridget's car. Slightly startling her, she turned around, and saw her mother. "Mom!" Bridget excitedly said, concurrently with a sigh of great relief, as she exited the car and threw herself into her mother's arms.

"Bridget, what in the world?!? I heard the news that there was a big storm. I've been trying and trying to reach you. I even called the police in your area! They said that someone had made contact with you, that you were ok, and should be on your way... but then you never showed up! Bridget, it's been over twelve hours. You had us all so worried."

Bridget pulled back from her mom and noticed her younger brother, dad, and some cousins who were all heading out of the caretaker-quarters, which was a 3,500 square-foot, white, ranch-style home with a two car garage. "We were totally freaked out, Bridget... Why didn't you call?" Bridget's mom wasn't going to let up until she knew the whole story.

"Mom, it's a very long story, and one I think should be discussed at least somewhat in private." Bridget said, looking at everyone who was now quickly crowding around her.

"Who is he?" One of her young cousins questioned loudly. Liam stepped out of the car, timidly holding the game Tyrnia had given tightly against his chest.

"This is Liam." Bridget said, not wanting to explain yet, till she found more information. "I'm watching him for his mom for a while. He's going to spend Christmas with us. I'll explain more, later." Bridget said, having motioned for Liam to come over to her, and putting her arm around him and squeezing him affectionately.

"Then let's go inside and talk and hear what happened." Bridget's father, Glenn Buchannon, stated in an official, organized, commanding tone, putting his arm around Bridget, to lead her into the house. "Any friend of Bridget… is our friend, too" he said, leaning in front of Bridget, directed at Liam. "We would love to know all about you, and are happy to have you join us."

"Thank you Grandpa!" Liam said, realizing that this was Bridget's dad. Since she was his aunt, and Bridget had called her mom his grandma, he did this innocently. He was not realizing or thinking of the fact that they knew nothing of the situation, and was simply excited that he had a grandfather he was getting to meet, who might be nice to him. Glenn's eyes grew huge as he froze, and stiffened up a little. Gina's face was equally as dramatic and contorted with surprise.

CHAPTER 29

"So you need to be clearer, Bridget." Glenn said with exasperation in his tone. In a secluded office-area of their family's home, Glen continued his understanding of the situation. "All you are explaining to us is that you dropped your phone, it was raining in a huge storm, and some crazy woman – who committed some serious crime, and isn't allowed to even touch, or visit her kid, or her abusive-husband came with the police and somehow knew that it was your house that they were going to! Somehow, it seems normal to you. Somehow, any of this makes sense?"

Glen ran his fingers through his now sweaty and ruffled hair. "And somehow... they let her bring a game with her, which might be a bomb for all we know by the way, and you believe her wacko story?! So you actually believe that she's your older sister, and that she hid stuff in your house a long time ago, to give you answers?! And this doesn't sound odd, or maybe even slightly delusional to you?"

"Ok, when you say it like that, it does sound extremely strange, and doesn't add up all the way. I get what you're saying, dad, but I also can't explain that somehow I know it's true. Dad, it was like looking in the mirror! I know she's my older sister. I can't explain it all the way, but..." Bridget paused and looked at the floor, trying to understand and think it all through, but also knowing what she felt and knowing what she experienced.

There had been a lot of tension and raised voices for a while, Liam sat out in the living area with the cousins and extended relatives. They all tried to make small talk as they tried not to listen in, but could hear bits and pieces of the loud conversation, through the glass office doors.

"Gina, I think you better shed some light for us here." Glenn turned to his wife out of frustration and confusion, knowing that his daughter was not one to lie or be dramatic.

Gina looked at her daughter, then her husband. "First I want to say, Bridget, I'm so glad that you are safe. I had many fears running through my head and was rather terrified! Second, I want to say that you don't know all of the details of your mom's life. You know... the things that I'm not proud of? Your dad does! Even though I can tell he's questioning me and concerned right now. Glenn, I have told you everything about me." Gina paused and swallowed hard, looking up to the ceiling, fighting back tears.

"Bridget, I had an abortion when I was 13 years old. It was twins, a boy and a girl. I was already 7.5 months along, but I almost died. The doctors convinced me to abort, I didn't want to. There is hardly anything in this world that I am less proud of. I wish with all my heart that I hadn't listened to them... That I could go back and undo watching his dead fingers and her fingers still wiggling... and her gasping for breath as they placed her body into a plastic bag to suffocate her.

I screamed and cried. I pleaded and begged, but they would not listen to me. I had already signed the paperwork. "I already gave birth to them and I'm not dead, you told me it would kill me and them!" I screamed at them. "I want my babies, they shouldn't have to die. Don't let anyone hurt them, the way they hurt me!" I plead as they took their bodies away from me, and shot me up with something that knocked me out, because I was 'out-of-control', in their eyes."

"But this Tyrnia cannot be mine. When I was older, 27 years old, I gave away a son, not a daughter. I put him up for adoption because I was in a terrible, abusive relationship and didn't want another abortion, but couldn't put him through life with a father who didn't want him or me. It was a closed adoption and I have also always been disappointed about that, as I met your father only 5 months after giving away my son."

Gina rested against the desk in the office after pacing around as she exposed some of her tragic and traumatic past to her daughter. "But I just don't understand, because he didn't look anything like you as a baby, and he was definitely a boy. I don't know what he looks like now, of course, or if he dresses as a woman, but you said that this Tyrnia is a girl, who had a son. And her son Liam, he must be her bio-son because I will say, Glenn and Bridget, that Liam looks almost exactly like my brother Hal. He died when he was around Liam's age. I know that somehow it must be that Tyrnia is related, or at least Liam is, because when he walked in here, I thought I was seeing my baby brother."

"Well, maybe somehow Tyrnia..."

Bridget was cut off by the phone ringing. Gina answered the phone. "Hello!... Yes, this is Gina Buchannon. Oh, yes, thank you Officer Fernandez, my daughter did finally arrive, just a little while ago. Sorry I forgot to call back and let you know. Thank you for checking with us." Gina was about to hang up.

"Wait mom! Don't hang up, please. Let me talk to him for a second."

"Officer Fernandez, my daughter Bridget whom you met, wants to talk to you for a second. Is that alright?"

Gina handed the phone to Bridget, Bridget motioned for a pen and paper. "Yes, hello Officer Fernandez. Yes, I'm fine thank you. Oh, I haven't even gotten to charge my phone yet, or check it, but I'm actually wondering if I could possibly get the contact information from you for the woman that you guys had with you, Tyrnia?"

"I don't understand Officer! Yes, the woman who you let come over to talk to us, while you were outside getting my phone." There was a brief pause. "What?!? I still don't understand. There was no woman?!? Then who were we talking to? Where did the game come from?" It was quiet on Gina and Glenn's side and they were extremely perplexed and concerned about their daughter.

"Oh, ok... No, I'm alright. Just a terribly long day, I guess. No, no problem, I'll talk to you later. I mean, hopefully not, I mean... ok, thank you, have a good day."

"What in the world was that about?" Glenn questioned. Bridget became a bit pale and frozen. Bewilderment covered her face.

"He said that there was no woman. He dug the game out of a hole, under the boardwalk. He found it alongside my phone. It had been triple wrapped and duct taped in plastic bags, so they un-wrapped it to see what it was. Once they realized it was harmless, they brought it to me. They had thought maybe it was some sort of weapon before that." Bridget pressed on the temples of her forehead, rubbing them gently. "I think I need to go to bed!"

2719

Esther Smith
Occupation: **Author**
Age: 40
Birth Gender: Female
Natural Hair Color: D. Bro
Complexion: Medium
Personality: Unknown
Married: Yes
Children: 8

WORLD CATALOGING PROGRAM

ONE ORDER

Esther Smith
Occupation: **Illustrator**
Age: 35
Natural Eye Color: D. Bro
Education: BA in Visual Communications
From: Alaska
Hobbies: Nature, children, art, photo restoration & more

CHECK OUT THE "NOVEL GAME"
@ WWW.ORDEROFUTOPIA.COM
AND OTHER ITEMS INCLUDING:
* MEET THE CHARACTER BIOS
* BOOK PREVIEW
* ABOUT THE SERIES
*UPDATES ABT. NEW BOOKS & PRODUCTS
* T-SHIRTS, PENS, ITEMS FROM THE BOOK, & MORE

www.ingramcontent.com/pod-product-compliance
Lightning Source LLC
Chambersburg PA
CBHW070616310726
48982CB00001B/98

* 9 7 8 1 5 9 4 3 3 9 9 8 1 *